ASHLEY BEEGAN

Mother... Liar... Murderer?

This book is dedicated to my amazing parents for always believing in me.

I'm sorry for throwing my uniform in the canal, and for everything after.

Love you always.

Contents

Prologue

Summer didn't know why Eddie was so upset with Mum. The door sounded like it would come off the hinge any second. She looked around, desperate for somewhere to hide.

'There, Summer!' Mum pointed to the table at the back of the lounge.

Summer rushed to the table, her legs wobbling like the jelly at Becky Smith's birthday party last week. She crawled underneath, bumping her head on the chair. A ten-year-old was far too big to climb under tables. This time was different, though; this wasn't a game of hide-and-seek. She regretted pulling a sickie from school now. Even putting up with the nasty jeers of Patty Whileman would be better than this. Mum ran to the table too and yanked down the checked tablecloth to cover the gap between the legs.

'Come and hide, Mum!' Summer raised her voice over the shouting coming from the other side of the front door. She couldn't quite hear what Eddie said, but he definitely wanted Mum to answer the door — that much was clear. Mum's pretty face popped under the tablecloth.

'Listen, Summer. Whatever happens, you stay there and you stay silent.' They had only just eaten lunch, yet her slurred words and blotchy skin showed she'd already drunk a sizable amount of vodka.

Summer nodded so hard that her head ached when she stopped. She put a hand to her forehead, closed her eyes and wished for Daddy to come back. It was silly. People didn't come back from the dead. Even so, it might happen if she wished hard enough. None of this would be happening if he hadn't died. She would be in school. Mum wouldn't slur her words. Eddie wouldn't be trying to kick in the front door.

Mum slid something hard along the floor to Summer and disappeared again behind the tablecloth. Summer looked down as the thing bumped her leg. Mum's mobile phone lay there, a quiet voice coming from it. She reached out, but just as her fingers tightened around it, Mum's face appeared again. Summer dropped it. She should never touch Mum's phone.

'Here!' Mum whispered. Summer snapped her head back up, hoping she hadn't been caught trying to pick up the phone.

Mum held something out to her. 'Take this and stay on the phone.' Mum was breathless now. She'd stopped slurring; her eyes were wide.

Summer didn't ask questions as she took the large kitchen knife. She wanted to but Mum's eyes scared her. Her face disappeared again. Summer held the knife with the blade facing away, like Daddy taught her when he showed her how to chop vegetables. She could still hear a voice coming from the mobile phone. She picked it up with trepidation.

'Hello?' she whispered.

'Hello, who's this?' The woman's voice sounded surprised.

'Summer. Who are you?'

'Well, Summer, I'm Suzie. I'm going to get you some help, OK?'

Summer nodded, feeling a bit too scared to answer. She didn't see why they needed help. Eddie was mad again. She knew he would just punch a wall or something and calm down.

'Summer, are you there?'

Oops, Summer had forgotten Suzie couldn't see her nodding. 'Yes,' Summer whispered into the phone. She wasn't sure why, but it seemed right to whisper.

'How old are you, Summer?' Suzie asked.

'Eleven in two weeks.' Summer refused to say she was only ten. She basically was eleven already.

'OK, sweetie. You're doing great. Where are you and your mum?'

'I'm hiding under the table. I don't know where Mum is.' Summer listened for a sign of where Mum was. She could hear her shouting to Eddie to calm down. It sounded like she was by the front door, which he was still kicking ferociously. 'She's talking to Eddie.'

'Eddie? Is that your brother? The one who is unwell?' There was a nervous edge to the lady's voice that hadn't been there before.

'Erm... yes. Eddie is my brother. I don't know what's wrong with him,' Summer whispered, 'Mum says he's poorly, but he doesn't seem sick; not even a fever. He just acts weird sometimes.'

'Is Eddie inside the house?' The lady sounded calm again.

'No, but he's trying to get in. I think he'll break the door down.' The door really sounded like it was going to splinter any minute.

'OK. Don't panic, sweetheart. The police are on their way. They'll be there in about five minutes, OK?'

Summer nodded again and kept listening out for Mum. She

3

wanted the lady — she'd already forgotten her name — to stop talking so she could listen and see what Eddie was so mad about. Why did they need the police? Eddie would shout and bang and hit the wall and then go away. She couldn't see why the police needed to come this time. Maybe he had hit someone else's wall. That would get him in trouble. He had been hitting things since Daddy died. Summer's heart hurt at the thought of her dad. She wished hard again for him to return.

Her eyes flew open as the door splintered. Mum screamed and ran through the living room and into the kitchen. Eddie's shouts were a lot louder now.

'Summer, are you still there? Summer?' The lady on the phone was talking, but Summer couldn't speak. Her body tingled with something. Not the sadness she'd felt when Mum told her Daddy was dead. An unfamiliar feeling that made her want to run away or scream. A terror she'd never experienced before.

'Mu-um! Where are you?' Eddie's deep voice laughed as he sang for their mum.

'She'll be in the kitchen, Eddie,' Marinda said. She was inside, too.

Summer filled with hope. If Marinda was here then maybe everything would be OK. She could see Marinda's white trainers by the living room door. Summer shifted forward, ready to dash to Marinda and ask her to make Eddie OK again. But then she spotted a larger pair of trainers. Eddie's black trainers. He crossed the living room floor, still calling for Mum. In seconds he was standing right next to Summer's hiding spot, and the police were nowhere in sight.

Astrid

It's a terrible thing to grow so accustomed to fear that it becomes a friend. When its welcome shadow reminds me to triple check I locked the door every time I leave the house. Or to look over my shoulder every three minutes to make sure nobody is following me. Or to text Harry at 11:55 a.m. every day, to check he's OK. A day without this shadow would be so strange. I wouldn't know what to do. Where would I go? What would I say? And if I didn't hear those constant warnings, what would keep us safe?

But on this particular Tuesday, my fear was far worse than usual. It wasn't the same nagging anxiety which kept me on my toes and ensured young Harry and I were safe. No. My friendly fear had manifested into full-blown terror because of a simple piece of paper. My trembling fingers made the scrap of paper shake, as if it was scared too. *Scared of me? I wouldn't blame it.*

Pushing the unhelpful thoughts away, I opened my fingers and watched the paper spiral to the marble table, which took centre stage in the kitchen. I picked it up again and threw it on the counter, where it sat ominously, a white warning against the dark quartz worktop. I stepped back, not wanting to be too close. My boots were loud against the porcelain floor. I stared at it from a distance, just to make sure it was real. Sometimes I saw things I knew deep down weren't real. Dark shadows who haunted me. Creatures that visited my nightmares. Quick flashes of movement in the corner of my eye, or a familiar face lost in a crowd.

I resisted the urge to move the paper a third time. Evil emanated from it, though I knew that was ridiculous. I was unsure why I had appointed human feelings to a piece of scrap paper. Where did it come from?

The note was waiting for me when I returned from the school run. Like flowers from a murderous stalker. The morning had started off normal enough. I'd walked Harry to school as usual and said goodbye with a quick hug before he crossed the main road. He sauntered the rest of the way alone, one shoelace trailing behind him and his black school bag slung over his shoulder. I rushed back due to rain drops breaking through the grey sky. I counted the seconds as I walked and checked behind me every time I reached one hundred and eighty. Sometimes I cheated and looked earlier, but one hundred and eighty was the magic number.

I used to walk Harry all the way to school, but he was fighting for independence lately. Eleven years old was far too grown up to be seen walking to school with his mum. At least it was in his mind. Not that you'd think we were mother and son. He didn't have my red hair or freckles, and he was already almost the same height as me. He looked like his dad, though Harry had never met him. His dad had been tall, with brown hair. Just like Harry. He had unblemished skin which tanned every summer within minutes of the first day of sunshine. I was grateful Harry didn't look like me. At least he wouldn't get bullied for being pale and ginger.

The walk back from school had been normal, too. I stopped off at the local shop for milk and made my way back to our traditional red brick home on Rose Way, a beautiful street on the outskirts of the small city of Derby. Tall oak trees lined the pavement, and each detached house had its own private gateway, surrounded by tall fences or trees. Privacy was the reason I'd been so eager to move into this house eleven years ago. The owner allowed us to move in with no credit checks or paperwork, thanks to a mutual friend. With four bedrooms and two bathrooms, the house was far too big for Harry and me. Nonetheless, I loved it.

Nothing felt different that morning. I thought I had such *good* instincts because I was always on edge. I would know if Harry and I were in danger again and I could prevent anything bad from happening. Yet my instincts must be waning after eleven years of being safe, because everything felt so *normal*. That was the worst part.

It didn't feel normal for long, though.

As I pushed open the front door, something underneath made an unusual swishing noise, like letters on the mat. But the postie always used our beautiful wooden postbox at the end of the garden path. I hadn't locked the front gate, though. I never did for the school run. It took less than ten minutes and even I wasn't that paranoid.

I closed the door, bristling at the thought of the postie missing the postbox. I gently placed my costly handbag on the coat rack and glanced at the mat. It wasn't the post. It was just a lone piece of white paper.

Even then, I assumed it was some sort of advertisement, which made me bristle further. We had clear signs on both the gate and the front: 'No Cold Callers' and 'No Unsolicited

Mail', yet the odd flyer still made its way through. It wasn't until I picked up that seemingly harmless scrap paper that I finally realised things were absolutely not normal. Nor would they ever be again.

Summer

I parked in the furthest space possible to make sure no patients could see me through the barred windows. I never liked patients to see my car if I could help it. Far too many of them had boundary issues.

I'd been waiting for this moment for almost twenty years, and yet I couldn't move. I wished my younger brother, Dylan, was with me. He was the only other person who would understand how I felt, though he would have talked me out of it.

I stood next to my car. The driver's door was open in case I ran away instead. But the previous month's events proved I couldn't run from the past any longer. I had to face it at some point. *Why not now?* Marinda had pushed me to this moment, regardless of what I wanted. I had no choice other than to seek Eddie out; I had to know the truth about him after what she'd admitted. I just hoped I wasn't putting my family in danger.

The autumn sun shone between the dark clouds. I covered my eyes to take in the vast building that stood before me. Sunlight sparkled on the raindrops which clung to the bricks after the recent downfall. It made the building less ominous, at least. I couldn't imagine this facility looking inviting in the dark. The council responsible for building the hospital years ago had buried it deep in the Derbyshire countryside. Field after field surrounded it in all directions, with various animals dotted around inside them. The countryside had never attracted me. It was pretty enough, but it bored me too quickly. The fields, trees and hedges all looked the same. A ten-foot wall barricaded the building inside a nine-acre space. A large sign read 'Welcome to Adrenna Hospital'.

It looked more like a prison.

Butterflies took flight inside my stomach as I made up my mind. I slammed the car door; the noise echoing through the silence.

After grabbing my handbag and laptop from the boot, I crunched over the gravelled car park to find the entrance. To start with I had to figure out how to get inside. These places were never easy to get inside on the first visit. I never knew why, but the entrance was never where you'd expect it to be. There were steps leading to the front entrance of the building, but the doors were barricaded with aged wooden boards. So I walked down the side and spotted a door with a cracked sign above it saying 'Welcome'. The butterflies got worse as I reached it. Another sign on the door informed me to press the doorbell. I squeezed my eyes shut. The image of the doorbell danced around on my eyelids, taunting me. *It isn't too late to drive away.*

'Can I help you?'

I whipped open my eyes at the sound of the crackling voice. 'Er... yes... hi...' I stumbled as I turned to see who had spoken, still jumpy even with Marinda locked away and awaiting trial. Nobody was there. It took me a moment to realise the voice came from the intercom system above the doorbell.

'I'm Summer Thomas, the advocate?' I said.

'Have you got your ID?' the woman replied.

'Er… yes.' I grabbed the ID card hanging around my neck and held it out to the intercom.

'Turn to your left, please.' Her voice made it clear she was getting agitated with me. I did as I was told.

Seconds later, a loud buzzing noise rang out and the lock clicked open.

'Please open the door and make your way to reception.'

I eased open the door as if something might jump out at me. As soon as I entered the hallway, my breath caught in my throat. That hospital smell of medicine, bleach, and disease hung in the air. An open stairway greeted me to the left, and a corridor stretched out in front of me. The decor didn't help my breathing. Deep red walls encased the entrance hall and the wooden floor was almost as dark. Everything you'd expect from such an old mental institution. Which was everything it shouldn't be in modern times. Dark, and sad, combined with a feeling of being watched at all times. My eyes flicked over the walls but I didn't see any CCTV cameras.

There was a door at the end of the corridor. I took my time to reach it, stepping carefully to quieten the heavy thud of my boots. Through the door, I easily found the reception desk to my left. It was as out of place with the old-fashioned decor as an iPod would be at an antique teapot display. It was such a bright shade of white that I had to stop myself from shielding my eyes after being in the darkness of the corridor. An authoritarian receptionist sat behind thick safety glass. She looked me up and down as I walked over to her, her lips pursed. She was clearly the same chirpy character from the intercom.

'You're not the usual advocate.' She clipped her words, as if she'd had enough of advocates already today, despite me being the only one. She raised a perfectly plucked eyebrow over her sizable glasses. Red lipstick smudged above her top lip. I tried not to stare at it.

'No. She's off sick.' I gave a friendly smile to win her over.

'Well, she usually comes on a Friday. Why don't you come back then? The residents don't like their routine being disturbed.'

My smile hadn't worked.

'I can't make it on Friday, I have my own visits to make.' I kept smiling and hoped she believed my lie. Sweat beads formed on my forehead. Christ. This battle-axe must scare the more anxious patients half to death.

'Well, it's only 9:30, most won't be awake yet.' She sighed. 'Sign in here, please.' She rammed a register under a gap at the bottom of the safety glass.

I did as she asked and pushed it back through the gap. My hands trembled. I cleared my throat loudly to divert attention away from them. She peered at me over the rim of her glasses and snatched the register back from the gap.

'Here are the keys.' She handed me a black pouch and a belt. 'And here's a locker key. No phones, handbags, laptops or lighters. You can have a pen and paper, but keep the pen out of reach. Don't put it down anywhere. Put everything in locker twelve please.' She pointed to the lockers behind me.

I nodded through her speech — I'd heard it all before at many other hospitals — and picked up the key and pouch before she changed her mind or asked more questions. I was lucky she didn't call my employer to check Becky wasn't off sick. I just hoped they assumed it was a daft mix up.

Once I'd put my belongings inside locker twelve, I turned to her, awaiting further instructions.

She said nothing, but stared back with one eyebrow raised again.

'Where are the patients?' I asked.

'Up the stairs, you'll find three doors. One for each ward.' She pointed back down the corridor I'd just come from and turned away to face her computer.

Without another word, I returned to the staircase and made my way up each step, gripping my pen and notepad as if they were weapons. I supposed they could be in the right circumstances. Especially a pen. The landing at the top had three doors, just like the old grouch had said. One door led to the left, one straight in front and one to the right. They were modern, with thick glass panels so anyone could see what was going on before opening the door. I peered through the first door on my left and saw another long corridor. It was the same through the second door. Through the third door was a large room with light walls and a white floor. Sofas and chairs were dotted about the middle of the room and a large TV was attached to the far wall, encased in a protective cabinet.

Close to the door a man in a white coat stooped over someone sitting in a chair. I fumbled with the keys, trying to find the right one to get into the room and wishing I had more of a plan. I hadn't really thought I would go through with it; expecting the hospital would turn me away. Or I'd run away myself. Yet here I was. *What if Eddie recognised me? What would I do if he didn't recognise me?*

Once I'd finally found the right key, I creaked open the heavy door, attempting to be inconspicuous. The man — I assumed he was a doctor — whipped around. He smiled at me, revealing blinding white teeth.

'Hi!' He was so cheerful I had to fight the urge to turn and

13

run.

'Er... hi. I'm Summer. The advocate.' I smiled back.

'Oh! No Becky this week?' he asked.

'No, she's off ill.'

'Oh, nothing too serious, I hope. I'm Dr Randall. Has anyone shown you around yet?'

I shook my head.

'OK. So this is ward C. This is Damon.' He pointed to the large man in the chair. Damon didn't move. He stared at the floor in front of him, ignoring us both. 'But... he isn't feeling too well today. I'll be back in a few minutes, Damon.'

He moved over to the far side of the room and motioned for me to follow. 'This ward is for the patients who are new to us and are very ill. Ward B is the next one along, and those patients have settled in nicely and are doing better. Ward A is for people getting ready to leave. So, just be most careful in this ward, as there are a few people you shouldn't be alone with. Avoid one-to-one with anyone in here today. I assume you know what you're doing.' He smiled again. His friendliness made him instantly likeable. I was always a little jealous of people who found it so easy to talk to people. I didn't even want to lie to this guy. But I had to.

'I think Becky had a meeting with one patient in particular today... Eddie?' I said.

He scrunched up his face in thought. 'Erm, Eddie... Eddie... ' he muttered. 'No, we don't have an Eddie in this ward.'

'It could be because his birth name is River.' The words came out too fast. Shit, I was forgetting my play-acting in my rush.

'River?' His eyebrows raised. 'I'd definitely remember that name. Nope, sorry, not in this ward.'

'What about the other wards?' I said.

14

'There's definitely no River in them either. Or Eddie anymore, for that matter.'

'Anymore?' I asked.

'We had an Eddie Thomas. He wasn't one of mine, but I do know we released him about six weeks ago,' Dr Randall said.

'Released?' Fear twisted around my gut. If they had already released him, he could be anywhere. He could know where Joshua and I live. He could pay a visit to Mum and finish what he started. She still lived in the same house he'd attacked her in all those years ago.

'Yes.' The doctor smiled. 'I believe he's in a low security unit now. I don't think I'm allowed to reveal which one to an advocate?' He posed his question with his head cocked to one side.

I looked away from Dr Randall, as if surveying the ward. It always annoyed me how little doctors knew about advocates. Could I lie to him? I needed the information, but I already might get sacked if Becky found out I visited and mentioned it to her supervisor.

'No. Not without the patient's permission.' I decided to tell the truth.

'Ah, fair enough. I assume Becky will be back shortly?'

'She will. She may even be in on Friday. I'm covering today, just in case. I'll have a chat with some patients. I'll stay in this area seeing as I don't know them very well.'

He nodded and walked back to Damon.

I wanted to leave straight away, but it would seem suspicious. And I couldn't leave without taking my things from locker twelve, right in front of the witch downstairs. She would definitely suspect something if I rushed off.

So I wandered away from Dr Randall and looked around the

15

open living area of the ward. I wished I'd taken my suit jacket off and left it in the locker. My nerves were already making me sweat more than usual, and the warm air exacerbated it further. The room smelled of sweat and something else I couldn't quite put my finger on, bleach maybe. There was one large window on the far wall, but it was firmly closed and, most likely, locked. As stifling as the air was, the atmosphere was colder than most of the hospitals I visited. Or maybe that was just my mood.

But an idea came to me. If the doctor couldn't tell me where Eddie went, maybe one of the patients knew.

The living area was quiet, though. If I was going to find someone who knew Eddie, then I needed patients who were less catatonic than Damon. There was an art room to my left, and a corridor leading off to what was probably the bedrooms. The only two patients I could see other than Damon were sitting on the sofa watching TV. Maybe they could tell me where Eddie went. I walked over to sit on the sofa across from them. They both eyeballed me as I sat down.

'Hello,' I smiled, 'I'm Summer, an advocate. I'm here to chat with patients. If you need anything…'

Their eyes were distant and unfocused, and they said nothing in response. The tall, slender one closed his eyes and rocked back as he fell asleep. I noticed purple bruising around his neck. The other man was short and stocky, with thick glasses and a bandage around his head. He stared in my direction though he didn't appear to see me, never mind hear my introduction. Christ, what drugs were these guys on? They were clearly not going to tell me anything. But I continued to sit and watched the ward instead.

A couple more patients appeared as the morning progressed, and I moved over to another seating area to introduce myself

16

again. But after an hour of the same distant look from every patient, I decided it was time to leave. Maybe Swanson could help me find Eddie. It would be a good excuse to call him, seeing as I hadn't heard from him in a couple of weeks. My butterflies returned at the thought of his voice. I silently shooed them away.

I headed over to the nurse's station to let them know I was ready to leave the ward. The station was a small room at one end of the ward, which was surrounded by thick glass. I peeked through the glass to see who was inside, and a friendly face stared back at me.

Aaron Walker.

Finally, someone who could help me.

Astrid

The sun struggled to shine as I sat in the back garden surrounded by plumes of cigarette smoke. My finger repeatedly tapped against my cheek as I allowed the burning smell to envelop me. I hadn't smoked for six months, but the note scared me more than the risk of lung cancer, despite my mum's slow death thirteen years prior. Not that I stuck around to watch her die.

I'd tried to ignore the note. I binned it and sat in my studio corner of the living room to concentrate on work instead. There was an editing job I needed to finish, as well as an illustration job. I had to stick to deadlines tightly, with word of mouth being my primary source of advertising. My high standards meant customers must book at least four months in advance and brought in more high-paying jobs than ever before. As I stared at the letters on the page, I knew I wasn't editing to my usual high standards. The note twisted around in my mind and swallowed any other thoughts like a dark mist. *Where did it come from? Who wrote it? What did they mean?* I needed a break.

So now it was early afternoon and the note was back in my hand. The corner stained a deep orange from old spaghetti bolognese. At least my hand no longer shook. The nicotine had calmed my nerves. I inhaled another lungful of the harsh smoke. It felt good as it hit the back of my throat. I held it for a moment before blowing out one long stream of smoke into the cool air.

Despite my fear, I couldn't stop looking at the note. It was like watching a horror movie. I wanted to look away, yet I couldn't. I *needed* to see what damage it caused. Except this was real life, our life, and I couldn't turn it off if it got too scary. I could throw it away again, but what would come next?

The paper wasn't big. It was torn, plain white paper. The writer had been in a hurry, judging from the scrawl. It could have come from my printer. *Maybe it did.*

I shivered even though there was no evidence that the sender had entered our home. Yet they *had* been in my garden. They knew where I lived.

I couldn't understand how. Nobody knew where Harry and I lived now. I had been in Rose Way for over a decade, so the odd person had visited. My landlady... although I saw her all the time as a friend, and she had no reason to threaten me. I discounted her. Alex Swanson... he had always protected me. I hadn't seen him in years, and he had no reason to threaten me. I discounted him.

A couple of Harry's school friends and his school records, I supposed. Then there were companies like the bank, the doctor. But nobody truly *knew* who I was. They knew me as Astrid Moor, with no knowledge of my past. Except Alex.

The note contained thick, black letters in sprawling hand-writing like a child's. Four short sentences. The words were simple, yet they surrounded me with a dark fear. Which I guessed was the wordsmith's aim.

The truth you must tell,

To all who you know,
Or you'll end up in hell,
Where you will never grow.

No one in my current life could have written this. They didn't know my truth.

I had worked hard to seem like a normal, straightforward person with no secrets in my past. Nothing to hide. A single mother; young, but not too young to raise an eyebrow. No dad in the picture. A decent income from reputable sources; paid her bills on time.

Only one past event could be connected. One event which changed my life and defined it in a way that I didn't realise a single misfortune could do.

And that was the mystery of my missing husband, Benjamin Bates.

Sophie - May 2007

S ophie forced a cough to shift the burning at the back of her throat. She loved the high. She usually enjoyed the burn, too, but this time it was stronger than normal. Where the hell had Mel got this cocaine? The thought didn't linger. As long as she got high, it didn't matter where it came from.

It was lunchtime and Mel *still* wasn't home. She disappeared with some random guy last night, after the club kicked them out at closing time. Luckily, Mel was coherent enough to give Sophie her house keys so she had somewhere to sleep. She'd have been fucked, otherwise.

Sophie stretched out on the sofa and wrapped the itchy blanket around her bare legs as she waited for the high to kick in. She preferred the sofa to Mel's spare room. Bedrooms were too personal. They were safe places for treasured possessions, or cuddles, or sex.

Mel's disappearance wasn't unusual, so Sophie didn't worry. But she was running low on the free gram of cocaine Mel had given her. She scrolled through her phone contacts, searching for someone who might have more drugs. It didn't have to be coke. She wasn't picky, just no heroin. As long as she didn't go that far, she'd be fine. Guilt twinged at her, but she knew she would survive long enough to sort out her shit. One day she'd be clean with a good job, a husband and some kids and she'd say a big 'fuck you' to Mum and stupid Greg.

That day wouldn't be today, though.

Three loud bangs on Mel's front door made Sophie jolt up. She ran her fingers through her long hair, trying to get the knots out whilst attempting to gather her thoughts. Should she open the front door? It was Mel's house, not hers. Another bang at the door. *Shit.* Annoyance flashed through her as she wished they'd fuck off and leave her in peace.

Although it might be someone with more drugs.

She stepped around empty beer cans to the front door, wearing only her t-shirt and underwear. She smiled to see she had left the keys in the lock the previous night. Or that morning, whatever time she made it home. She opened the door a crack. A tall, skinny man stood there in dark tracksuit bottoms and a baggy t-shirt. His jaw swung from side to side. Sophie dropped her smile as she realised his jaw swinging was him chewing gum, and not the effect of drugs.

'Hey. It's Ben, right?' Sophie had met Mel's older brother a couple of times. He was a plumber or electrician or something like that. And quite sexy in a wiry way, at least compared to all the drug addicts around town. He had muscular arms for a skinny guy, and eyes which were almost grey. Sophie noticed his hands more than anything else. Big hands that would make anyone feel safe.

She smiled up at him and hoped she didn't look too rough. Mel had mentioned he'd asked about her. She'd told him to fuck off and leave Sophie alone,. Actually, Sophie didn't mind his attention. She opened the door wider to show him what she was wearing. Or, more accurately, what she wasn't wearing.

'Er… hey, Sophie.' His eyes flicked down to her bare thighs like she'd hoped.

'I guess you're here to see Mel? She's not in yet from last night. I'm not sure where she went, so I don't know when she will be back.'

'Oh. Er… OK.' He didn't move, but stood and stared at her instead. She couldn't tell whether his eyes were actually grey. His gaze flicked down to her loose breasts. Her nipples had hardened from the cool breeze blowing through the front door.

'She probably won't be that long. Do you want to come in and wait? We could have a drink together? I just took a line and need someone to party with, anyway.' She winked at him and immediately regretted it. Winking was never sexy in real life. What the fuck was she doing? She laughed. A buzz was flowing through her brain, messing with her thoughts.

He grinned, despite her lame wink, and nodded in return. Sophie walked away, taking her time so he could look at her arse. It was her best asset; the only part of her body she liked.

The cocaine swelled her confidence and she swayed her hips as she avoided the empty beer cans strewn across the living room carpet. Not the sexiest atmosphere. It would have to do. She turned as she reached the kitchen. He whipped up his head with a guilty look.

Sophie pretended she hadn't caught him staring at her arse. 'What do you like to drink?' A wave of excitement flowed through her.

'Er, anything. I'm not picky.' He threw his phone and wallet down on the kitchen table.

Bet you're not, she thought as she bent over to open the fridge door.

23

'Do you prefer Carling or John Smith's? Or Mel might have some vodka knocking around somewhere.'

'Carling is fine. I don't do bitter and vodka makes me angry.' His jaw twitched.

'I know a few people who say that about vodka. I don't think any alcohol makes me angry.' She took her time to grab a four pack and smiled as she passed him the beer.

'Break me one off,' she said as she walked back to the living room. There was only one sofa in the small room. She sat in the middle.

She eyed him as he lumbered over. He had a strange way of walking. It was as if his legs had grown quicker than everything else and he was still getting used to them. She enjoyed the vulnerability of being half naked while he stayed fully clothed. There was something sexy about being so exposed, and the possibilities of what might happen next.

Greg had always liked it when she was naked and he wasn't.

She tapped a chipped fingernail against the small bag of white powder on the table and raised one eyebrow at Ben.

'No thanks, beer will do me. I don't do drugs.' He eyed the bag as if it were a bomb. Ben's strong South London accent made even simple things he said sound cocky. He exuded confidence, even without drugs. It intrigued Sophie, maybe even made her a little jealous.

'Suit yourself.' She flicked on the TV to remove the possibility of an awkward silence. On the news, a reporter showed an image of a nearby street where a teenage girl was raped. That was not the sexy atmosphere Sophie was looking for. She switched to the music channels. Music was always easy to talk about.

'Leave this one on!' He took a seat next to her. The song was

24

a heavy rap song Sophie had never heard of.

She laughed as he attempted to rap along, losing the pace within seconds.

'Stop laughing at me. I bet you can't do better.' He continued his attempt to rap, nodding his head in tune with the music.

Sophie laughed harder.

Over the next hour, they finished their pack of beer and attempted to sing. Ben gave her a disapproving glance but said nothing as she snorted another small line of white powder. Sophie felt the heat from his body as they moved closer together.

The drug coursed through her body, her confidence rising, and her inhibitions falling away. A need to touch him overtook her. She placed her hand on his thigh. A slow smile spread across his face, and he leaned forward to kiss her.

His tongue was rough in her mouth. Sophie didn't mind. She needed him to be rough. She needed him to take control so she didn't have to think anymore. He pulled off her t-shirt and pushed her down onto the sofa. His large hands cupped her breasts and squeezed hard, just like she'd been imagining since he sat down. It hurt more than she expected, but she didn't care. It was a nice pain. His stubble scratched against her neck as one hand pulled down his tracksuit bottoms. She was barely wet when he pushed himself deep inside her and moaned into her ear.

Five minutes later, it was all over. Sophie lay naked on the sofa in his arms. She would be happy with her accomplishment until the drugs wore off. Ben's heavy breathing drowned out the noise of the quiet music coming from the TV.

'I'd better go,' he told her ten minutes later. 'I don't think Mel would be too happy if she saw me here, lying naked with you.'

'Oh, OK.' Sophie smiled and rolled away from him to grab her t-shirt and underwear from the floor. 'I need a shower, anyway.'

'Yeah, you do!' he grinned. 'How old are you? You never said.'

'I'm eighteen.' It wasn't exactly a lie. It'd be true in a couple of months.

He picked up his jacket and phone, and threw her an awkward wave as he strode out of the front door and slammed it behind him. Sophie lay on the sofa, grabbed the scratchy blanket, and went back to scrolling through her phone. She would find someone more fun than Benjamin Bates. It was the only way she knew how to stop the loneliness from winning.

Astrid

I struggled to concentrate on an illustration for a children's book. It crossed my mind that a run might clear my head more thoroughly. I hadn't run for three days, and it was a necessary evil to stop the fear from growing too big. The darkness struggled to keep up with me when my feet hit the ground until they ached and my lungs almost burst from my chest. It always returned soon after I stopped running, but as a smaller, manageable darkness instead of the intense demon it sometimes became.

Even so, I wasn't in the mood for running, and I needed my fear with me today. I had a reason to be scared, and I needed help to deal with it. The fear would keep me alert. I couldn't forget that.

At 2 p.m. I gave up working and sat in front of my new laptop. The sun disappeared altogether and the grey sky made the day even more depressing. I sat in the garden with the laptop, regardless of the weather, hoping it would clear my head. And I sank into the hanging egg chair that Harry had made me buy the previous summer. The fresh air felt cool against my skin. It was a welcome refreshment.

At three grand, the laptop was an expensive treat, but one I needed for work. Then I spent another thousand on Harry's new laptop to bring him out of his recent pre-teenage funk. I regretted the spend because it depleted my emergency fund, which I usually made sure totalled at least five figures.

I never knew when we would need to disappear.

Still, just under eight thousand was enough to escape should we need to, though hopefully it wouldn't come to that. I pulled the elastic band around my wrist and let it go. I snapped it again and again. My anxiety lessened with each snap of pain. I stopped and counted to ten before snapping it another three times. I needed to get stronger. That *poem* was going to force me to do something I hadn't needed to do in years: check up on my relatives.

My usual work-related social media account popped up. It displayed happy pictures of a young woman I'd never met. A stranger I befriended on social media, then stole her photos and blocked her and her entire friend list. She could still catch me, of course, but she hadn't found me out so far.

But that wasn't the account I needed to use. I logged into my other account. This time a man around my age smiled at me from the profile pictures. He was attractive, whoever he was. I had created the fake male profile after Harry and I left our old life, when Harry was only a few weeks old. I'd added over two hundred strangers as friends. Then I added the people I wanted to monitor. People who could make my life very tricky if they wanted to.

I had three prime suspects for the sender of the note. They were not the most intelligent people in the world. So I prayed that whoever had sent the note was a social media over-sharer. I genuinely hoped to see 'Haha put this note through her door today.' written on somebody's account.

By relatives, I didn't mean my blood relatives. I didn't know any of my own relatives. I'd only known my mum, and she'd died before I got married. Not that she would have been welcome at the registry office. She'd chosen Greg over me a long time ago, and I hadn't seen her since I was 15. That was sixteen years ago No, by relatives, I meant Ben's family. My in-laws, though I supposed they were nothing to me since his disappearance. It took a couple of tries to remember the password. Once I'd logged in I searched for my sister-in-law first, Mel Bates. Her round face smiled as her profile picture pinged up. Yellow hair fell limp around her shoulders, hiding most of the tattoos covering her arms. Like most profile pictures, it was about as far from the truth as you could get.

Anger bubbled inside me as her blank eyes stared out. I felt a petty urge to write something unpleasant beneath her picture. I snapped the elastic band against my wrist three more times. *Stay calm.*

Other than her marriage, Mel's life had changed little in the last decade. We last saw each other just after our friendship fell apart, when she was a single mum to baby Jayden. Since then, she had married and given birth to another son.

I scrolled down through her last few posts. They were mundane and mostly food related. I stopped scrolling on the fifth image. It was a picture of *three* young kids with the caption 'mummy luvs you more than anything xxxxx'. Jayden was about Harry's age, and the younger boy looked about six. The little girl looked no older than a toddler.

I continued to snap the elastic band. I could never understand how someone like Mel could create child after child, whilst I would never have another. She shouldn't be allowed one child, let alone three.

Still, nothing about a note or any ominous statuses that could be about Harry or me.

Fear gripped me before I'd even finished typing the next name in the search bar; I knew what I was about to see. She hadn't changed her profile picture in years. As her profile popped up, I came face to face with the very person who haunted my sleep. Julie Bates stared out at me with an enormous smile and wispy brown hair, but it wasn't my mother-in-law I was afraid to see. She wrapped her arms around a teenage version of my ex-husband, Benjamin Bates. Ben, who I had loved more than life itself, and who now lived in my dreams as an emaciated and rotting figure.

Julie had been my second biggest enemy, ever since Ben and I moved away to escape Mel's attempts to break us up. It was Ben's idea to move. I'd have done *anything* for Ben. Yet Julie had always blamed me. She didn't realise it was her own clinginess and Mel's lies that he needed to get away from.

Julie hated me enough to want to scare me, or worse. If she knew where I lived, she'd be straight round banging on the door and causing trouble with her big mouth. But she wasn't clever enough to figure out where I was, or to write a threatening poem. I doubted she could even spell after so many years of alcohol abuse. I scrolled through her profile. There were no posts, just game notifications filled her feed.

I moved on to the last candidate. I'd left my enemy number one until last because I needed to build up to it. To remind myself he wasn't the little boy I'd fallen in love with anymore. Ben's oldest son, Kai Bates, would now be about twenty years old. A well-timed breeze made goosebumps appear across my arms as I opened Kai's profile. I slammed down the laptop screen before it could load, delaying the moment I might see his face.

I sat for a minute before meandering back inside to the warmth of the house. I poured a glass of water on my way to the living room, procrastinating as much as possible. Eventually, I curled up on the Arlo & Jacob sofa in the far corner of the living room. I wished I had wine instead of water but pushed myself to focus. There were no harboured bad feelings from me towards Kai, although I couldn't imagine he was a pleasant person after being dragged up by his awful mother. I did know he would blame me for taking his dad away, thanks to his mum and grandma telling him their version of events.

Once curled up, I couldn't delay it any longer. I held my breath, and pulled open the laptop screen. Kai's profile showed nothing. The profile picture showed some random singer or rapper, and the banner was a black logo I'd never seen before. I released my breath, and scrolled through his feed. He had posted nothing for months. Harry told me kids these days only used certain social media apps, and others were for 'old' people like me. It was funny, I didn't feel old. I felt like my early thirties was a weird age category: neither young nor old, but not middle-aged either. Though to eleven-year-old Harry, I may as well have been one hundred years old.

Kai remained my best guess. His youth suggested an awareness of technology that made him more likely to know how to find me, despite how careful I had been. At least if Kai wrote the note, Harry was safe. He wouldn't want to hurt his younger brother, who was innocent in the whole thing. Harry didn't even know Kai existed, and I was going to make sure it stayed that way. There was only one person I knew for sure had not written the note, and that was Ben himself.

Because I murdered him eleven years ago.

Swanson

Detective Inspector Alex Swanson poured over the thick file at his desk. The pounding in his head had increased, and the fumes of fresh white paint did not help in the large, open office. The peeling, grey walls had been fine as they were in Swanson's opinion.

There were more urgent things to spend time and money on. A third sexual assault had taken place in the city centre within six months, and they needed all the possible funding to find the depraved arsehole.

The office buzzed with activity, with more officers roaming around than Swanson had ever seen, and the noise was making his head worse. He rubbed his eyes and blinked hard at the file in front of him.

The victims had all given a similar description of the rapist. He was white, about six foot with dark facial hair and a prominent nose. No tattoos or anything of much use, and no DNA so far. The first victim, nineteen-year-old student Lu Chen, had showered before arriving at the station the day after the attack. She said the attacker smelled of petrol and had a foreign accent, though she didn't know where from.

The second twenty-one-year-old victim, Donna Bradway, got away by kicking him hard in the balls and screaming '*fire*'. She'd read somewhere that people are more likely to pay attention if you scream 'fire' rather than 'help'. To be fair to her, it worked. A couple came running to help her, but the suspect had disappeared by the time they arrived. She said the attacker smelled of paint and his accent was like a mixture of Russian and French.

The third victim was still being interviewed by a specially trained officer.

A TV appeal with a facial composite would go out on tonight's news. It was going to be a long week of looking into the plethora of mostly useless leads from the public. The first attacks both happened in the depths of the picturesque former mill village, Darley Abbey, on the west bank of the River Derwent. The third took place close to the university grounds. Swanson was waiting on the interviewers to confirm exactly where.

Footsteps moved towards him, and he smelled a puff of sweet scent as DI Hart flopped into the chair on the other side of the desk. She sighed.

He didn't look up, so she cleared her throat. 'I can see you grinning to yourself about ignoring me, Alex Swanson,' she said in mock exasperation.

'I'm busy.' Swanson dipped his head further, though he still grinned.

'Uh huh. We will be after tonight.' Hart sighed again.

'You not looking forward to the prank calls?' Swanson finally looked up at her sharp face, which was expertly painted as usual.

'Shut up.' She rolled her eyes. 'We'll hopefully get some sort of lead. I've been thinking about petrol and paint. Why would he smell of both?'

'Well, could be anything really, couldn't it? He might have filled his car up recently and spilled a bit. Like when you spilled some on your shoe.' He laughed at the memory of her panicking about catching fire.

'Oh, fuck off,' she mumbled.

He stopped laughing. 'What's up?' he asked. Hart was usually quick with the banter. Just telling him to fuck off was a failure in her eyes.

'Nothing other than this rapist.' She put her head in her hands. 'He's ruining my comeback game.'

'We'll get him.' Swanson's tone was serious.

She looked up at him in surprise.

'Yeah, we will.' She smiled. 'I need a wee.'

'I didn't need to know that.' Swanson shook his head as she got up and walked off.

She had a point about petrol *and* paint. Were there any jobs or hobbies where you might smell of both?

He closed his eyes, but the noise of everyone milling around and talking drilled into his skull. He needed to get out and away from the mess. Quiet spaces were far better when he was working through a problem. He crossed the office, dodging DCI Murray's view, and climbed into his black Audi in the rear car park. He could go home for an hour and have a working lunch there, although it would be a late lunch as it was 3 p.m.

He weaved in and out of the mid-day Derby traffic and onto the A52, heading four miles east to his home in Ockbrook. He felt the tension ease as he left the A52 and drove along the quieter roads of the small village. His cottage was behind a Moravian Church, one of very few Moravian settlements in the UK.

He pulled up in his driveway and kept his head down, not

wanting to catch the eyes of any neighbours as he hurried to the tired front door. Moving away from his mother would be best. It was only stubbornness that kept him in the village. Why should he be the one to leave? He had moved away for a bit, but that didn't turn out well. Now he lived right behind the highly religious Moravian settlement his mother was a part of. Not that he had anything to do with her or the church. Atheism was more his style.

His cottage had no entrance hall, and the front door opened straight up into the wonky living room. It was his favourite room in the house because it had everything he needed. His telly sat on top of a modern oak TV stand, with a PlayStation underneath that Hart ripped him mercilessly about on the few occasions he had allowed her in his home. A mini fridge that housed energy drinks and chocolate sat next to the ancient sofa. The previous occupants had left the sofa, and it was the comfiest sofa Swanson had ever owned. It was covered by the blanket he slept under when he couldn't be arsed to go upstairs to bed. His weights sat in the adjacent corner, though he hadn't used them in a week. And if he needed anything else, the kitchen was only a few feet away and had a small toilet squished in under the stairs. Other than using the shower, he barely needed an upstairs. The only problem with the living room was the low ceiling when he was working out. Either his fist or his head was going to go through it one day.

He sat on the sofa and pulled out a notebook and pen from underneath. He made notes on what he knew so far and what he didn't yet know. After shaking and scribbling the pen to get it to work, he noted the suspect's description, accent, and the distinctive chemical smells outlined by the victims. That he legged it as soon as the second girl fought back showed he was a wimp and likely to be some sort of social outcast. But it wasn't definite. People had easily fallen for Ted Bundy's charm, including the judge who sentenced him to death. This guy hadn't killed his victims, though. Not yet. So the major concern was escalation. If they didn't catch him, his confidence would grow and the level of violence would probably escalate.

It was unlikely that the first victim was this guy's first crime. He probably started off with something far less risky. So what was he doing until the last six months? And where? What if he had been doing this in another location? Swanson grabbed his phone to call Hart.

She didn't bother with 'hello'.

'Er, why are you calling me? Just come and speak to me. I'm still in the office,' she said.

'I came home for a bit to think.'

'What the?' He could hear Hart moving as if she was looking around for him. 'Oh, that's why everyone is much happier than usual.'

'Hart, listen. I think this might be someone who just moved into the area. We agree these aren't likely to be his first victims, right? He probably started off smaller.'

'Right,' Hart said slowly.

'Well, what if he's just moved to Derby?'

'From a different country?'

'Well, I was thinking from a different town, though I suppose given the strange accent it could be a country.'

'I'll ask Murray what we're doing about cross-referencing similar crimes nearby. I'm sure she's got some guys on it already. Are you coming back in?'

'Yeah, yeah. I'll be back soon.'

He hung up and admitted defeat to the pain in his head.

There was an old box of paracetamol in the also-wonky kitchen. He downed a couple of pills dry, then sat back down and closed his eyes, waiting for the pain to go away, but his mind glazed over. And he never made it back to the office as promised.

Astrid

My ex-husband didn't disappear. I murdered him after an argument. Then I hid the body in such a wickedly clever place that nobody would ever find it, and cleaned the scene so comprehensively that I left zero evidence. All while looking after a newborn baby. It really was a miracle. At least, if you asked Ben's family, that's what they'd tell you. But there are many sides to every story, and you should never listen to just one if you want the truth.

My phone vibrated in my pocket. I took it out and threw it on the black glass table in front of me. I would have been in trouble if Harry saw, after telling him to be careful with the glass table many times over the years. The sun returned once again, and shone through the window to bounce off the screen of my laptop. Typical autumn weather. I shifted my position on the sofa to face away from the window and continued to scroll through social media.

All that appeared were the usual self-serving and attention seeking statuses. I never understood why people are so desperate for attention and 'likes'. It all seemed so fake. Harry wanted to be a scientist when he was little. Thanks to *influencers* he now wanted to be a millionaire YouTuber. Personally, I'd prefer to stay in my own world and speak to nobody except Harry ever again. I stopped scrolling and slammed the laptop screen down before throwing it to the other side of the sofa.

I perched on the edge of the seat with my head in my hands and eyes closed. Someone was fucking with me, and I needed to find out who. I was so lost in my thoughts that I didn't think to check my phone. Fear gripped me as the noise of someone yanking on the handle of the front door filled the hallway. I froze, listening for further noise. There was only silence. I shook my head; I was hearing things.

Then the banging started.

Someone was trying to get inside my house.

My heart thudded as I jumped off the sofa and ran into the corridor, stopping dead in the doorway to the hall. Nobody *ever* visited us unannounced. Nobody knew where we lived. So who the hell was banging on my door?

I pulled at the band on my wrist, hoping it would help to stop my panic from spiralling. It didn't work this time. The door handle rattled again as someone pushed against the door. I stepped away and backed up until I was in the kitchen. *Should I get a knife? Should I call the police?*

The darkness began in the corner of my eye. It always started there. I needed to calm my anxiety or the darkness would creep out into the room, seeping into the ceiling next. That's when the fear Arracht would appear. My very own monster. But I couldn't lose myself in the darkness today. I had to find the person who wrote the note, and I couldn't do that by hiding.

I pulled the elastic band harder, but the quick flash of pain wasn't enough to drag away the darkness. My panic had grown too quickly. The door banged again, and I ran to the far end of the kitchen. I crouched on the floor, nestled into the corner.

It felt the safest place, and my legs were weak from fear.

The darkness seeped into the room as I knew it would. The corners of the kitchen ceiling turned grey at first. A fuzzy grey, like when an old TV loses signal. I closed my eyes and hummed. I didn't want to hear the guttural sound of the Arracht. It would reverberate off everything around me and stick in my brain.

Yet, through the darkness, a glimmer of determination reached out to me. I could not let the poem undo all of my hard work. That was what the sender wanted, and I refused to let them win so easily. I opened my eyes and forced my legs to stand. The movement made the blood rush to my head. My vision quickly went dark, and the kitchen turned sideways.

At first I thought the Arracht had arrived, silently for once. After a few seconds, the kitchen righted itself and my vision cleared. I stumbled to the kitchen doorway and leant against it, to flick the band against my wrist in quick bursts of three. This time it worked, and the pain absorbed my anxiety. I walked to the front door.

And then the yelling started.

Sophie - June 2007

It took three hours to decide on the little black dress from New Look, and now Sophie regretted it. It was far too short and men kept looking over, making her even more nervous than she had been on the walk over. She hoped she looked old enough to not be asked for ID in front of Ben. That would be seriously embarrassing. Luckily the bouncers let her straight in.

The smell of beer hit her the second she walked into the pub. It was more of a local drinking hole than a place to go for a proper night out. It surprised Sophie to see so many people inside on a Saturday evening. There were mostly groups of drunken men dotted around on various tables and bar stools. Some turned to stare at her, but she was careful not to return any looks so she didn't lead anyone on. There was only one person she was interested in seeing tonight.

The noise from other punters faded as Sophie spotted Benjamin Bates sitting alone at the table nearest to her. She'd never seen a cheesier grin than the one on his face at that moment. She grinned back at him and walked over.

'Hi,' she said, as she sat across from him and placed her bag on the chair next to her.

'Hey. I got you a beer.'

Ben pointed at the pint sitting in front of her and she took a sip, wishing she knew what to say on a date. What did people on TV do?

'So, have you been here before?' he asked. He looked down at his own pint and fingered the rim of the glass.

'Yeah, I've been here a few times with Mel and a few of the other girls,' Sophie said.

Ben's grin dropped as soon as she mentioned Mel. *Shit*. Had she just ruined her first date within the first five minutes? 'Have you been here before?'

'No, but I've heard Mel talk about it. She said it's one of the less shitty pubs.' He looked up at her and his grin returned.

'They make nice food,' Sophie said, her panic over and lesson learned. She wouldn't mention Mel again.

'Do you want to eat? I'll buy you something. What do you want?' He reached for his wallet.

'Oh no, I don't want anything. I was just saying.' She laid her hand on her stomach to stop it rumbling as he counted the notes from his wallet.

'No, no. If you want food, I'll buy you food. Do you want chips? Shall we share some chips? Yeah, we'll share some chips,' he decided for them.

Sophie laughed.

She studied him as he walked to the bar. His cocky stride and confident grin hid a sweet awkwardness. She tried not to think about Greg. That bastard had hurt her enough, and there was no way she would go back after he chose her mother over her.

'Cheer up, it might never happen.' Ben's voice shocked Sophie out of her trip down memory lane.

'Oh, sorry! I didn't see you coming.' Sophie tried to laugh it

42

off.

'No seriously, what's wrong? Have I upset you?'

'No. Definitely not. I was just thinking about something.'

'Was it your mum?' Ben asked.

'My mum?' Sophie stared at him.

'Yeah… sorry, I shouldn't have asked. Mel said you haven't seen her in like a year. I was just being nosey, I guess. I'm sorry. You don't have to tell me anything.'

'No, no. It's OK. It's just that people rarely ask me about it. I think they find it awkward to ask.'

'I have a habit of speaking before I think. I hope I haven't upset you?'

'No. I'm fine. And no, I haven't seen her in a while. I moved out after she chose her boyfriend over me.' Greg choosing Mum over her would be more accurate, but she wasn't having Ben think she was a slut.

'Parents suck.' He reached over and took her hand. Her dainty fingers disappeared in his fist. 'I'll take care of you.'

She laughed. Ben didn't. His face was serious. 'I mean it, Sophie. I'll take care of you, if you let me.'

'I don't need taking care of, but if you're offering…' Sophie laughed and ignored the nerves creeping in, because she knew that within those opening minutes of their first date, she had fallen in love with Benjamin Bates. And love never ended well for her.

Astrid

'Muuuuuum!' Harry yelled through the door. 'Open the door for God's sake!'

In all my years of being a mother, I'd never been so relieved to hear him yelling my name in such a pissed off tone. I sprinted to the door to let him in.

'What the hell are you doing here?' I said, embracing him the second he got through the door.

'Er, school finished.'

I let him go and he grinned up at me, clearly finding the situation hilarious.

'Jesus, Harry, you should have called! You aren't big enough to cross that main road by yourself.' I couldn't help but raise my voice.

He laughed at my shock. 'You shouldn't be late then! I can't just stand across the road waiting for you like a five-year-old.' He rolled his eyes, as did I. He may not look like me, but he certainly had the same attitude I had as a kid.

'Just call me next time!' I said. I let him inside the hall and closed the front door behind him.

'Oh, so you're planning on forgetting about me again then?' He raised his eyebrows.

'What? No! Of course not. I'm sorry, baby. Come here.' I

kissed his soft forehead and squeezed him tight again.

He allowed it for a second. I breathed in the soft scent of his shampoo and felt my anxiety dissipate. Then he shrugged me off like he always did lately. I looked away so the hurt didn't show on my face. He was growing up, and that was a good thing.

'It's OK, Mum. I enjoy walking on my own. I'm going upstairs to watch YouTube.' He kicked off his school shoes, leaving them a foot away from the shoe rack, and ran up the stairs to his room.

I didn't bother to tell him to put his shoes away properly. Instead, I watched him disappear around the corner on the landing, my heart still thumping. As soon as he left I pinged the elastic band on my wrist, closed my eyes and imagined the panic draining away. Harry was fine. I made one mistake after a terrible day, and I won't let him down again. I'll order his favourite Chinese food for dinner as an apology.

Feeling calmer, though still shaken, I locked the front door and pushed the handle down three times to make sure it wouldn't open. In the kitchen, I made sure I'd locked the back door as well. Again, I rattled the handle three times to calm the fear, even though cameras lined our front and back gardens. I returned to the living room to carry on my research.

Cameras lined our front and back gardens.

I slapped my forehead. How could I have been so stupid? The note had turned me into a gibbering mess. I grabbed my phone. Harry had texted me to say he was walking home and my guilt increased. I shouldn't have ignored it when Harry relied on me to be a good parent.

I opened the camera app and scrolled through the saved recordings, searching for this morning's visitor. The camera recorded every bird that flew by, every car driving past the front, and every cat that visited the garden. So there was a lot to scroll through to find the visitor.

I scrolled right down to 8:35 a.m. and watched Harry and I leave for school. A minute later, a boy not much older than Harry rounded the corner and stopped outside our front gate. He looked left and right before slipping through the gate and running up the drive with something white in his hand. I felt nauseous looking at this intruder on the drive, despite his young age. He disappeared briefly as the porch overhang blocked the camera's view, before he left the garden round the same corner he came from.

I rewound the recording back to where he stood at the gate, looking straight at the house, and I zoomed in on his face. His pale face was clear, as were the accompanying pimples and the scrap of paper in his hands. But I didn't recognise him at all.

The fact that it was a child made it somehow worse. I hadn't expected to see Mel or Kai sauntering down my drive with the note in their hand, nonetheless I had at least suspected to see an adult. A child surely wouldn't write such a threat and post it through the door. Then a realisation hit me that made the darkness rush at me once more. Maybe I was wrong, and the threat wasn't related to me and Ben. Maybe the note was for Harry.

'Never again will you grow.'

Summer

Aron sat opposite me, sipping fresh coffee in a small cafe belonging to a farm, only ten minutes from Adrenna hospital. He ran his long fingers through his floppy black hair, as he often did when nervous. I fingered the glass of cold water in front of me. It had only been six hours since I'd seen him in the hospital. Apart from the drizzle of rain against the windows, and the chatter of a nearby family, the silence hung in the air between us.

Not that long ago our bodies were curled naked around each other. But we hadn't seen each other since his release from hospital just over a month ago. I wanted to give him space and time to heal after what Marinda did to him and his mother. I also didn't know what to say to him, and he didn't call me either.

'So, Summer Thomas.' He smiled at me. I missed his smile. His pale face lit up from even the smallest smirk. 'How have you been? How's Joshua?'

'Joshua is great. Cheeky as hell. He's at my mum's house at the minute. I'll pick him up when we're finished, seeing as I'm done working for the day. I'm OK, too.' I paused and smiled, not sure what to say next. Our eyes locked, and I cleared my throat and looked away. 'You have a new job then?'

'Yes. I couldn't go back to Derby. I know Marinda isn't there anymore, but still. Too many memories. And I didn't want her knowing where I worked. I've moved house too.'

'Where to?' I asked.

'Nearer to Adrenna.' He looked away.

I didn't push him further. Maybe he didn't want me to know either.

'So how long have you been working at Adrenna?' I asked instead.

'Not long. Two weeks now.' He slurped his coffee.

'Oh.' My smile dropped.

'What's wrong?' He put down his coffee and turned his full focus towards me.

'I was just hoping you could help me with something. It doesn't matter if you're so new.' I tried to hide my disappointment. He wouldn't have any idea where the hospital had released Eddie to. He probably didn't want to know anything about Eddie, anyway.

'Summer, you know I'd do anything for you.' He leant over the table and squeezed my hand, but caught himself and let go, clearing his throat.

I moved my hand back to my lap. 'Aaron, you've got a new job. A new home. You're still healing both physically and mentally, and I don't want to impede that. Anyway, I'm not even sure if I want to find him. It's feeling like all the signs are saying I shouldn't bother.'

'Find who?'

'Just a patient. It doesn't matter, honestly.'

'Another missing patient? I'm not going through all that again, Summer! And I definitely don't know anything this time.' He gave a hollow laugh.

'No! Not a missing patient.' I laughed too. 'Adrenna recently moved a patient to a low security unit. I'd like to know where he went is all. Just to see if we work with that unit. I wanted to check in on him.'

'Oh, well, that doesn't seem like a hard request? I'll just check the computer. It should say.'

'You're not allowed!' I protested.

'Who's going to know? I won't tell if you don't.' He shrugged. 'What's the patient's name?'

'OK. It's not *just* a patient, His name is Eddie Thomas.' I gave him an apologetic look.

His face paled. 'Eddie? As in Marinda's ex boyfriend Eddie?'

A protective instinct flared within me from somewhere. 'No. Eddie as in my brother Eddie, who Marinda fucked up so badly he nearly killed his own mother.' The words came out much harsher than I meant. I sighed and rubbed my face in my hands. 'I just wanted to see if he's OK. He's a victim too, just like you. He needs to know what Marinda did. He needs to know he didn't hear those voices, and that she was responsible for what happened.'

'He still tried to kill your mum, Summer!'

A few tables down, two children looked over at us. The parents tried to distract them with the menu.

Aaron lowered his voice. 'He's dangerous.'

'Yes, which is why I'm not sure I want to find him. But they've locked him away all these years, Aaron, and why? Because that evil woman took complete advantage of his fragileness after Dad died. He needs my help.'

'What about Joshua?'

'I won't let Joshua anywhere near him. I'll make sure of it.'

'Sorry, Summer. I can't help you. It isn't safe.' Aaron stood, his chair scraping against the floor. The family turned again to stare at us.

He walked away before I could reply.

I lowered my head to hide my flushed cheeks. Aaron's reaction wasn't a surprise. I couldn't blame him. There certainly wasn't much chance he would call me now.

I gave him a few moments to drive away and then walked out into the drizzling rain. I pulled up my hood, wishing I'd parked closer. Halfway down the street, I noticed Aaron was still in his car, engine on, staring out the window. He looked up and spotted me. Our eyes locked. His mouth opened as if he was going to say something, but he turned away and sped out of the car park instead.

I continued to my car, my heart heavy with guilt and annoyance. It was me who Marinda had wanted to hurt, yet it was Aaron who got caught in the middle and suffered the consequences. Him and his poor mother. But my brother needed me, too.

And DI Swanson was the only other person I knew who might help me.

Astrid

I tried to act as normal as possible that evening. I ordered Chinese food as a surprise and shouted at Harry to come downstairs once the food arrived and I'd set out his plate of chow mein.

'Look, your favourite!' I said, as I followed him into the kitchen.

His face lit up as I'd hoped. 'Thanks, Mum!' He grinned. He scraped the chair across the tiles as he sat down to eat. I winced, but clamped my mouth shut.

'How was school?' I asked instead.

'It was fine.' He shovelled the dripping noodles into his mouth.

'Careful! It's still quite hot.' I tried not to stare at him as I considered how to get him to talk. 'You do anything good at school?'

'It was school, Mum. Of course not.'

I tried a couple of times to get more than a few words out of him, but it was no use. He just didn't open up to me like he used to. We settled in the living room after our food, pulling out the recliners and watching the newest Ice Age film, sharing a bowl of sweet and salty popcorn. The film was one of a few favourites that he wasn't too old for yet. I glanced at him. He looked relaxed, lying back, his floppy hair hiding his forehead.

Yet there was something on his mind. We usually laughed and chatted together, and he had barely made a sound since the film started. Maybe he was mad at me for forgetting to pick him up but didn't want to admit it. Maybe he was just in a pre-teenage, sulky mood.

I could not mention the note. The words were far too haunting for an eleven-year-old to hear. I didn't want to scare him. But I had to find out if he knew that kid.

'Get up to much at break time?' I enquired, trying to sound light and carefree.

'What? No. Just a normal day.' He shrugged, still staring at the TV screen.

I tried again. 'What did you get up to?'

'Can't really remember.'

'It was only a few hours ago.' I laughed.

He shrugged again.

'Listen, when you won't talk to me it makes me think things *aren't* OK. You would tell me, would you? If you had any problems?'

'Of course, who else would I go to?' He gave me a look that asked if I was losing my mind. He was right. We had no one else, really.

'Well, there's Barb if you ever needed someone and I wasn't around. Do you have her number?' I suggested our landlady, my only friend.

'Yes, of course.' He looked away and back to the TV screen. 'I can't hear the film, Mum.'

I sighed but stopped talking. It was pointless. When he was smaller, I always knew what was wrong. It was me and him against the world after his dad's disappearance. I was honest with him and told him everything I could about Ben. Harry didn't seem too negatively affected by the whole thing, although it had to have an effect somewhere along the line. Now he was a pre-teen, it was becoming more and more difficult to know what he was thinking.

Could that note really be for him, though? The only thing I knew for sure was that I would not let Harry out of my sight until I found out what was going on.

The next morning, I got lucky and could put my plan into action straight away. Thanks to the pouring rain, Harry was happy to be driven to school and I didn't need to explain my sudden insistence that we drive there. We pulled up outside the entrance to the school.

'Want to stay in the car for a bit? It's still chucking it down out there.'

'Yeah, alright then.' He raised his voice over the rain hammering on the car roof.

'Want to play eye-spy?' My fingers drummed the steering wheel as I surveyed the school grounds in search of the boy who delivered the note. His pale face stuck in my mind.

'No, thanks.' His tone suggested he was unimpressed with my suggestion. 'Why do you still have the engine on?'

'So I can keep the windscreen wipers running.'

'Why bother?' His tone was still hostile.

'So you can see when your mates turn up,' I lied. I continued to survey the street, where everyone rushed by with hoods up and brollies open. It would be difficult, if not impossible, to spot the kid if he passed.

'Can I sleep at their house tomorrow night?' Harry asked, his tone lighter.

'Whose house?' I turned awkwardly to face him in the rear

seat.

'The twins, obvs,' he said, giving me a big smile. It was amazing how sweet kids could be when they wanted something. 'Please?'

'OK,' I said after a moment's silence. At least if he was at the twins' house he'd be safe.

'Thanks, Mum.' He grinned at me. 'You're alright, you know!'

I laughed and shook my head. We sat quietly, each lost in thought, and a few minutes later the hammering stopped and the rain slowed to a drizzle.

'I'm off, Mum.' Harry pushed down the car door handle.

'OK, babe. Be careful, won't you?' I replied, watching him through the windscreen mirror.

'Careful of what?' He threw me another exasperated look.

'Oh, you know, just in general.'

'Erm, OK.' He began to leave the car, then stopped and looked down at his feet.

'You OK?' I asked.

'Yes... Love you.' He ran out of the car and slammed the door shut before I could respond.

I smiled as I watched him rush over to the school gate with his head down against the trickle of rain still coming.

Then I saw a figure by the gate, and my smile dropped.

I craned my neck to get a better look. It was a man, dressed smartly like a teacher. But it wasn't a teacher I recognised. He put out a hand to stop Harry as he reached the gate, and though I saw his lips move, I couldn't make out what he was saying.

Harry turned back to look at me with a befuddled look on his face. A cloak of fear grew around me. Something about this man wasn't right. I rushed out of the car. As soon as I opened the car door, the man hurried away. Within seconds, I lost him in a sea of faces. I ran to Harry, still stood at the same spot looking at me.

'What did he want?' I was breathless by the time I reached him, despite only running from across the road.

'He asked if I know somebody called Sophie Hunting.' Harry shrugged. 'Weird, eh?'

I felt the blood drain from my face, and tried not to show my shock. The street spun. I grabbed the gate to steady myself.

'Mum? You OK?' Harry's worried face looked up at me.

'Er, I don't feel too good, to be honest, babe. Dicky tummy. Run off into school and I'll get home quickly. Don't worry about that guy and don't leave the school without me. I'm picking you up from the playground today.'

For once, Harry didn't argue. He just nodded and walked off. Though he kept turning to eyeball me as he walked away.

I smiled and waved at him until he disappeared, but the edges of my world were darkening. The street spun again as I whirled around to find the figure, though I knew he was long gone. I closed my eyes and made sure the spinning stopped before I fought through the crowd of kids, parents, and teachers. I couldn't spot him anywhere.

I stood still, looking at the streets he could have vanished down. There were so many possibilities. He would be miles away if he drove.

Darkness encased my vision, and I needed to get home to safety. I flicked my elastic band as best I could under the sleeve of my coat and took deep breaths as I hurried back to the car. I could see other parents and kids staring at me. I didn't care.

Once in the car, I threw off the coat, closed my eyes and flicked the band properly. When I opened them again my vision was clear, and I knew what I had to do.

I rushed back home and sat in my car for a moment to make sure the kid wasn't around waiting to deliver anything else. My two neighbours across the street were chatting in their respective front gardens, so I didn't sit in the car for too long.

I listened for the sound of another note as I opened the door. It relieved me to hear nothing, and I rushed to lock the door behind me.

I didn't bother trying to work this time. Instead, I used my laptop to look up estate agents, both in the area and further outside. I had money saved to move away. The tricky part was that I needed to rent and remain anonymous. The two requirements rarely went hand in hand. I rented from Barb because she was happy for me to give her cash in hand. There was no contract, so she hadn't formally recorded our agreement anywhere. I've never been sure what Alex Swanson told her to convince her to let me move in, to be honest. But she'd only ever called me Astrid. She didn't know the name I was born with.

Yet that man at the school knew my other name. Sophie Hunting.

Ben and his family knew me as Sophie Hunting, though I became Sophie Bates not long after we met. A little too soon, according to his family. The strange man not only knew this, he also knew Harry was my son. He must have seen me in my car with him. This stranger knew I would see him talk to Harry, and he must have had an escape plan because he disappeared within seconds. But that man wasn't Kai. So who the hell was he, and how did he know who I was?

The name change was all done legally by unenrolled deed poll, which meant no solicitor involvement and no public record. I had proof if I needed it, though other than travel I didn't need to evidence it much. No one should have been able to find out via public record. Yet someone *had* found me.

Even so it didn't matter. I could move house and get away again. I'd done it once, I could do it again. And this time, I had spare money, and an older child rather than a baby. I had far more experience of being a mother and an extra decade's worth of life experience. We could do it properly this time. We could start a new life somewhere amazing.

I could tell Harry I was making more money and wanted a bigger kitchen or more rooms. Maybe a games room; that might convince him. We could move to the beach. Harry loved the beach. Or even Scotland—although I'd heard it was always cold there. I hated being cold. Moving south might be nicer. It was expensive down south, but I could afford it thanks to my illustrating business.

I drove to school at 2:45 p.m. to wait for Harry. They didn't finish lessons until 3:30 p.m. but I wanted a spot right outside the front gates. Despite the fact it would upset Harry. He could have more freedom once we moved. That could be another thing to add to the bargaining chip.

I studied the space around the school, watching for the man to appear again. Half of me wanted to confront him, the other half wanted to never see him again. I supposed the best thing to wish for would be him disappearing and everything just going back to normal. I had to face the fact that was unlikely to happen. He hadn't appeared when Harry sauntered out of the gates at 3:40 p.m., chatting to Tom and George as he walked. The same friends he was having a sleepover with tomorrow night.

He saw my car within a moment of leaving the school gates,

so I waved at the three of them. His face dropped. He sloped into the car with his head down.

'I'm not that embarrassing, am I?' I smiled at him.

'Let's just go home,' he rolled his eyes.

I would have laughed if I wasn't so distracted, still searching for the guy from that morning. 'Anything else happen at school?' I asked in the most unassuming voice I could muster. I pulled off from the street and began the short drive home.

His head shot up from his phone. 'What do you mean?'

'Any more strange men asking if you know random people?' I eyed him through the front mirror as we stopped in school traffic, waiting for someone to let us out onto the main road.

'Oh yeah, forgot about him. That was weird!' He relaxed again.

'Yeah, it was. So, any more odd things happen?' It was like getting blood out of a stone. Something had made his head shoot up like that, though.

'Oh no. Just another boring day at school.'

'Why did you look at me so strangely when I asked then?'

'Because you're being weird and I didn't know what you were talking about!'

I couldn't disagree, so we drove the rest of the way home in silence. Driving was such a waste of time when it took less than five minutes, yet I felt safer in the car. It was a weapon, after all. More people probably died from cars than guns. At least in the UK. And I could put my foot down and just speed away at any moment.

A genius thought hit me: a camper van. It would be perfect! No one would ever find us. Would it be cool enough to convince Harry?

Once we reached home, Harry mooched up to his room

again to watch YouTube while I made dinner. I practiced the conversation in my head.

The campervan was one idea, despite how expensive they were. We could move to the beach, or near mountains. We could have a games room if we had a house. Then I hit on something I was certain would work. I'd always refused to buy him a dog, not wanting the additional responsibility if we had to move. But a puppy had a real chance of convincing him the move was a good thing.

I made Padella's pici cacio e pepe for dinner. Pasta was another of Harry's favourite foods. Cooking was never my strength, until Harry reached six months old and I realised I needed to reduce his milk and feed him proper food. I taught myself healthy cooking through online videos and now I was proud of my skills.

I called Harry downstairs once it was ready. Excitement coursed through me at the thought of his smiling face when I promised him a puppy. I flicked the band on my wrist three times, just to rid the last speckles of anxiety.

'Hey baby.' I smiled at him and kissed his forehead. 'Made your favourite.'

He beamed as he sat down to eat his pasta. I sat opposite and gazed at him for a minute before picking up my fork and shovelling some pasta into my mouth. I tried to gauge his mood, though I supposed it didn't matter either way. My appetite was humongous. It was the fear that caused it, feeding off my anxiety and causing my appetite to become insatiable.

I swallowed my pasta and smiled over at him. 'Harry, I have some exciting news.'

He looked up with a grin, pasta spilling from his mouth as he spoke. 'You're pregnant?' He pointed to my stomach.

I laughed. 'Harry! This is serious.' It was nice to see him with his sense of humour back.

'Oh no.' He rolled his eyes in mock exasperation and flicked his empty fork around. 'Go on then, break it to me.'

'I've had a fantastic idea. I got a big job and came into some money, and I think... I think we should use it wisely. Maybe we should move.' I let my words sink in before continuing.

His face dropped. He stopped eating his pasta and stared at me. I couldn't tell if he felt panic or anger. 'What? Why?' he asked in a small voice.

I cleared my throat and looked down at my pasta. The black cloud grew in the room's corner once again, darkening my peripheral vision. 'Well, I thought we could go somewhere amazing! Like the beach?' I smiled as broadly as I could and hid my arms under the table to flick my band.

'I don't want to live on the beach. It's for holidays. I don't want to move, Mum.'

'I thought you'd say that. Look, if we lived near the beach we could get a puppy. Any puppy you want. We'd be in the right area for one. There's nothing around here for dogs, but if we moved to the beach...?' I let my trump card sit in the air and prayed it would get the reaction I needed.

The silence became uncomfortable before he spoke. 'My friends, Mum... I don't want to move schools. I don't want to be the new kid with no mates.' His fork clattered as he threw it down onto the table.

'You hate school.' My anxiety was rising and the dark cloud now covered the entire kitchen door.

'I don't hate my friends, though.' He pouted and folded his arms across his chest. 'I wouldn't see them anymore.'

'If we moved, you wouldn't have to go to school.' The words

came out of my mouth before I had even considered them. 'You could learn from home and play the rest of the time. You could chat with your friends online and then see them on weekends. They could visit and you could visit them. It will be fine.'

'Why?' He looked at me, his eyes hard.

'I told you why. I just... it would be nice to live near the beach.'

'No. You've just promised me a dog and no school? You're desperate to move house suddenly. What are you not telling me?'

Sometimes I forget how grown up he was these days. Harry had spent his entire life in my company. He knew me better than anyone.

The shadow threatened to swallow me whole. I grabbed my skin and pinched, digging my nails in hard. Pain grounded me, and as long as I stayed grounded, the shadow would shrink again.

'Well, the big job I mentioned, it's in Cornwall.' I told him the first lie which came into my head. Anything to distract him. I was a good liar. I'd been lying about my identity for years.

'Ooh, so that's why you want to move. Just say that then, Mum. And I'll think about it.' He jumped off his chair and ran upstairs without even asking about dessert.

As soon as he left, the darkness shrank and I breathed a sigh of relief. The fear was often my friend, but when it grew too big, bad things happened. It had the power to take over everything, including my thoughts and actions.

I didn't bother to scold him for not putting his plate away as I usually would. I was glad he'd gone to think about it. He needed space to come to terms with what I was asking from

61

him. I'd planted the seed. All I needed to do was wait.

After washing up, I retreated to the living room and spent an hour looking at properties in Cornwall, which was expensive compared to Derby. I wondered how to rent a house without exposing my identity. I couldn't go to a normal estate agent. Surely that would be traceable? After some searching, I found a website featuring private landlords with empty properties. Still, it was risky. I'd have to meet them first to make sure I could trust them, and I didn't have time for that. Harry returned downstairs just after I closed the laptop.

'Mum.' His voice was barely audible as he stood in the doorway looking at the floor and twiddling his hands. He looked so small. 'I was thinking about what you said, about moving.' He looked up at me with sorrowful blue eyes. 'I'd miss it here.'

My heart ached for him. The one thing I'd vowed to give him was a stable home, after my shit show of a childhood. And I was failing him. 'Come here, baby.'

He walked over to me, and I squeezed my arms around him. A steely determination came over me as I breathed in his scent. How dare this stranger upset my child's life. I'd felt this familiar determination before. 'It's OK. We aren't going anywhere.'

Sophie - September 2007

Sophie curled into Ben's chest as they lay on his battered sofa, watching one of the gangster films he loved so much. The ones she pretended to love just to spend time with him. She breathed in his heady scent and cuddled tighter into his chest.

'Are you enjoying our first night living together?' He kissed her forehead.

'I'll remember this day and night forever.' She smiled back at him. *Fuck you Mum, I am happy.*

'Day?' He raised an eyebrow.

'Meeting Kai!' She moved back and looked up at him. 'He's gorgeous!'

'He's cheeky.' Ben laughed.

'Yes, in a gorgeously adorable way!' Sophie said.

'I'll always take care of you, you know that, don't you?' Ben's face was serious.

'Yes.' Sophie looked away and settled back into his chest.

'What's wrong?' Ben asked.

She hesitated. 'I've heard it all before, Ben.' She looked back up at him. 'Promise me you mean it?'

'You've heard it all before? Do you mean you heard it from Greg?' Bens' face dropped. 'He was a paedophile, Sophie. He

63

didn't love you. Not like I do.'

She tried not to react to the paedophile comment. She looked away, and her body stiffened. Greg wasn't a paedophile. They fell in love. The memory of Mum catching them having sex in the kitchen made her shiver. Everything was OK until that moment.

Except that didn't matter anymore. Not now she had Ben to look after her.

'Listen, babe. Greg was an arsehole. He used you. Anyone in their forties shouldn't be anywhere near a teenage girl.' Ben pulled her face to his and kissed her hard. 'See? *I* really do love you.'

'I love you too, Benjamin Bates.' She uncurled from his chest and straddled him instead. She pulled off her top and looked down at him. 'See? I'd do anything for you.'

They made love right there on the sofa. And as they lay cuddling afterwards, Sophie knew at that moment they were going to make it. He would never let her go, she'd make sure of it. Whatever it took.

Astrid

Harry lay in his bed, with the duvet half off and TV still on. Faint snores escaped his lips as I watched him. An urge to climb in next to him grabbed me, just like I used to when he was younger. He'd sneak into my bed in the middle of the night most nights until he was nine years old, but one day he just stopped. I couldn't even remember the last time it happened, or the last time he'd kissed my cheek.

I pulled his duvet over him before creeping out and into my own bedroom. My wardrobe area was just big enough to walk into, with lots of shelves to store various items. Or hide them, if necessary. I reached up to the top shelf to pull down a box, the contents of which I hadn't seen in a long time. I moved the box to my bedroom drawer for ease and slipped a heavy weapon I'd hidden into my handbag.

Back downstairs, I triple checked every gate, door and window before climbing into bed just after midnight. I flicked the telly on and surrounded myself in the duvet, tucking every part of the duvet around my body like a swaddled newborn. An old re-run of a game show played on the telly as I closed my eyes, hoping to drift off into a dreamless sleep.

A clicking noise woke me, and my eyes flew open. *Click, click, click.* The telly had turned itself off, as it usually did in the night. I tried to sit. My body wouldn't move. I knew that noise, and it made me sick with dread. *Click, click, click.* The sound was coming from inside the room, and it was getting closer.

Panic built within me. I called out for Harry. My lips moved, yet no sound came out. My breathing came faster; the only noise beside the clicking. I tried again to move my arm, but something was holding it down. Something was holding my entire body down. My vision was clear. The shadow of fear was nowhere to be seen, yet my panic turned to terror. *Click, click, click.*

The far corner of the duvet moved. I couldn't turn my head, and from the corner of my eye I watched a lump under the duvet moving closer to me. It moved a few inches, then stopped. Then moved another few inches and stopped. As it shifted nearer, I saw it was the same size as a cat. Each time it stopped, it would click. *Click, click, click.*

The mobile phone beside me vibrated. Someone was calling me. I desperately tried to reach out to answer it, but the invisible force on top of me was too heavy. I still couldn't move. Sweat dripped into my eyes. The creature was now right next to my leg.

I felt a sharp scratch against my thigh and tried again to cry out. The noise died in my throat. The creature moved up the bed towards my head. I turned my face away as much as I could. It rubbed against my arm, then stopped. The *click, click, click* grew even louder.

I squeezed my eyes shut and willed my body to move. Blood pounded in my ears as I fought against the invisible pressure.

Finally, my arm pinged free. I rolled out of bed onto the floor with a thump and grabbed the phone.

'Hello?' I gasped. I was almost hyperventilating.

I flicked on the light and flung the duvet off the bed. Though I knew the Moralia would have left. It wasn't the first time it had visited me, and it wouldn't be the last. Even so, this was the closest it had come to reaching my face.

A raspy breath down the phone was all that greeted me.

'Hello? Harry?' I said again.

I ran towards Harry's room to make sure he was OK, but froze at the whispered growl at the other end of the phone.

Tell Harry the truth about his dad, or I will tell him for you.

The dial tone beeped and I threw the phone away from me onto the floor. My breath came in ragged, quick gasps. I turned to continue down the hall and into Harry's room, my pyjamas stuck to me with sweat.

Harry was sound asleep, still bundled up in his Minecraft duvet. I forced myself to breathe deeper and flicked my wrist. His snores helped to calm me. I closed my eyes and imagined the panic leaving my body. I stood there until my feet ached and I could stand no more. It might have been two minutes or two hours; I had no idea. But then the tears came, and I had to leave so I didn't wake Harry.

I stumbled back to my bedroom on numb legs and recovered the stash of cigarettes from my underwear drawer. It took four tries to light the cigarette with my shaking hands; I leaned out of my bedroom window to smoke it. There was no way I was going outside after that phone call.

The cool night breeze on my face felt good. I took deep, slow drags of the cigarette and watched the smoke as it weaved against the moonlight before fading away.

Tell Harry the truth, the voice had said. It sounded male. Could it be the man from the school?

However, I'd always told Harry the truth about Ben. The only people who accused me of lying were those who believed I was a murderer: Mel Bingham, Julie Bates and Kai Bates. My three suspects.

The Moralia plagued me for months after Ben's disappearance, but this was the first time it had visited me in years. It only visited when I was stressed or scared. I'd never seen what it looked like, but I had named it after a mythical Slavic creature called Mora. Mora was a part human, part animal monster that would invade your dreams and sit on your chest so you couldn't move. But Mora was a myth.

The Moralia wasn't.

At least, not to me. I didn't want to sleep again. The Moralia couldn't get to me when I was awake. I needed light and noise, so I made a coffee and sat in the living room with the telly blaring and the lights turned up to full brightness. But the night's events had exhausted me and, despite the coffee, I drifted off into a dreamless sleep. I woke to Harry shaking me.

'Come on, Mum. We've got to leave for school soon,' he whispered.

'What? What time is it?' My brain was foggy. I yawned loudly and fought through the confusion at being in the living room.

'About eight! Why are you on the sofa? Why are you still asleep?'

'Oh, I didn't sleep well.' I waved him away.

'Is that why the lights are on? Did you watch a scary movie again? You shouldn't watch them!' He smiled at me, knowing how much of a wimp I was.

'No, I just had a silly dream.' I gave him a big grin to prove I was OK.

'Aw, well come and wake me next time you have a nightmare and I'll make sure you're not scared, Mum.' He surprised me by wrapping his arms around me in a bear hug.

'Thanks, kid.' I squeezed him back and kissed his cheek. I'd missed this side of him. 'Now let me go, I need to get ready!'

'I can walk on my own...' He said as he walked into the hallway.

'No, you can't!' I laughed at his hopeful face. 'Maybe soon, though, OK?'

'OK.' He grinned and went into the kitchen.

I rushed into the shower and dressed in skinny jeans and a tight jumper to block out the cool autumn temperatures. I dragged a brush through my hair and attempted a smattering of makeup so my pale face didn't scare anybody on the school run.

Harry made us toast while I sorted myself out. He was terrible at buttering, leaving two large clumps of butter in the middle rather than spreading it around.

'Wow, this toast is the best I've ever had!' I exclaimed as I forced one bite down my throat. 'Come on, we'd better drive so we aren't late.'

'OK, can you not park right in front of the gates?' he mumbled. My pre-teen was back.

'I'll park across from the gates, that's all I can offer.' I shrugged.

We rushed into the car but I was calm on the drive to school. This was not the time to risk a speeding fine. I didn't even look back at the house as we left. I dropped him off across the road and watched him walk into the school rounds. I waited until the crowd cleared, and there was no strange man to be seen. Once the school gates had closed, I left.

It wasn't until my return home that I noticed something was wrong. It wasn't obvious. I don't even know what made me look over as I got out of the car.

Our front garden was small. The driveway took up most of the space to the right, with a grassy area to the left. Lipstick pink Nerines lined the end of the patch of grass. Orange chrysanthemums grew next to them. Someone, or something, had flattened both.

An animal could have destroyed my flowers, but... all of them? Only a massive animal could do that.

A human being sitting there waiting for me, however, would be big enough. The raspy voice from the previous night echoed in my ears. Was he watching me when he phoned? Did he run away when I opened the window to smoke?

I glanced around, my body on alert, but the garden was empty.

It relieved me to find the front door still locked. Nobody could be inside.

I slammed and locked the front door behind me and completed my usual checks. I stood in the hall and listened for noise or any sign of an intruder inside the house. Silence greeted me.

I didn't bother taking my coat or shoes off and instead walked straight into the living room. Perched on the sofa, I pulled my phone from my pocket and opened the camera app. The camera footage rolled in front of me as I scrolled through every recorded movement. Nothing suspicious came to light. I threw the phone away, watched it skitter across the coffee table and skid to a stop against a coaster. I couldn't deny what was happening any longer. Harry and I were in danger.

I needed help, and I had only one person to ask.

Swanson

Swanson swore as he narrowly avoided a driver swerving into his lane. He considered pulling the idiot over to scare him a little and make him drive slower in the future. But he'd overslept by an hour, and he was late for work. His mobile phone rang, distracting him.

He glanced at the car dashboard to check who was calling. Unknown number. He ignored it but listened as the call went to voicemail, hoping the mystery caller would leave a message. Instead, the line went dead. Fine. They would call back if it was important.

The sun broke through the clouds, and Swanson pulled down his sun visor to shield his eyes. He didn't want to wear sunglasses in October. And the sun could get lost as far as he was concerned. The grey sky suited his mood better. His head was pounding.

Less than a minute after it stopped, the shrill ring of his mobile phone began again. He looked down. It was the unknown number. He sighed and clicked the answer button on the steering wheel.

'Swanson,' he muttered. The idiot driver still played on his mind.

'Hi, Alex Swanson? It's me.' A woman's husky voice filled

71

the car.

Swanson held back another sigh and fought the urge to ask who. It never went down well when he did that. Why did so many people expect him to remember them by voice alone? The huskiness awakened something in his memories, though. The female witness from last week, maybe?

'Er, hi.' He stalled for time.

'Hi, I'm sorry for calling, Alex, but I really need your help again,' she said, confusing him further. Nobody from work called him Alex. Even people in his personal life called him Swanson, other than Aunt Barb.

At the thought of Aunt Barb, the husky voice clicked in his memory. 'Sophie? Is that you?'

'Yes. I thought you already knew that?'

'No. It took me a minute to recognise you. It's been a long time. Sorry, what did you say you wanted?' Swanson kept his tone cool despite his surprise.

'I need your help.' She sounded on the verge of tears.

'Look, Sophie. I've given you enough help,' he replied calmly. 'You can't call me every time something goes wrong. We've talked about this. A long time ago.' He ignored the guilt which arose. It felt unnatural to push someone away who needed help, however he had no choice with Sophie Bates.

'I know, Alex. And I promise I tried hard not to call you, but someone is after me. I'm terrified.' Her voice wobbled again.

'Someone is after you? What do you mean?' Despite his reservations, his detective side couldn't help but ask questions. He spotted a shop and swerved into the car park, narrowly avoiding an old lady in a Nissan Micra.

'I got a note through my door the other morning. It told me to tell Harry the truth or I'll go to hell, and never grow. That's a death threat, right? I checked the camera and the person who posted it was some young kid. And then at the school run yesterday morning a random guy walked up to Harry and asked him if he knew me.' Her voice grew louder with each sentence.

'A child put a daft note through the door and then someone asked Harry if he knew you? It hardly sounds like someone is after you, Sophie.' He rubbed his beard and closed his eyes. He should have cut her off earlier. She always dragged him into her messes somehow.

'Yeah, well, my name isn't Sophie anymore, so why would they be asking for me under that name, Alex? And that's not it — if you'd let me finish. Someone called me last night from an unknown number and called me a murderer and when I woke this morning they'd been outside my house! They had trampled all of my flowers.'

OK. Maybe she really needed his help this time. 'Did you see them?' Swanson asked.

'No. I've checked the CCTV and I can't find any recorded footage of them, but if it was dark and they were slow enough, it might not pick them up. It's not great in the dark.' Her voice had changed to little more than a whisper. 'Something weird is going on, Alex. I need your help.'

The guilt grew, yet he knew he couldn't get dragged in again. He could lose his career, and then he'd be no help to anyone. 'Well, notes and anonymous calls aren't my department, Sophie. Call the actual police. They will help you, honestly. It's nothing to do with me.'

'The death of a child would be your department,' she spat and hung up the phone.

Swanson winced as the dial tone filled the car. The dull ache in his head had increased tenfold. Sophie always knew just how to get him to do what she wanted. But it wouldn't work this time. He wasn't falling for it. He dealt with enough nutters as it was, and it became a bigger part of the job every year. It used to be that people were criminals or they weren't. Now everything was all convoluted. It was a good thing for people who were genuinely suffering from mental health issues and needed help, but certainly made things more complicated.

He turned up the radio. Maybe noise would drown out his headache. He pulled away from the car park and resumed his drive to the office.

Unless it got dangerous, Sophie needed to figure this one out for herself.

Astrid

A mixture of annoyance and longing curdled within me like a nauseous cocktail of beer and wine. I knew asking Alex for anything again was a longshot, but I thought he'd care enough to help us. He was a bigshot detective these days, and it seemed he thought himself too important for Harry and me. Still, it was nice to hear his voice after so long, if only for a minute. He recognised me instantly, though I'm not sure he felt the same way about hearing my voice as I did about his.

I pushed my feelings about Alex to one side and concentrated on the next steps. If he was unwilling to help, then I needed another plan. Ensuring Harry's safety was my biggest priority. I didn't know if this person was a physical threat to Harry, but if they threatened a woman, it wasn't a stretch to assume they'd hurt a child.

I texted him and asked him to go straight to Tom and George's house after school for their sleepover. I knew their parents wouldn't mind giving him dinner. It was only a few doors down from the school and he'd walk there with his mates, so he would be safe.

Next, I called Barb. She was the closest thing I had to a real friend. I closed my eyes and prayed for her to answer the phone. She didn't work other than being my landlady, so she was often free unless getting her hair done or a facial. My prayers were answered after only three rings.

'Hey, Barb, how's things?' I stood up from the sofa and circled my living room as I spoke.

'Oh hello, beautiful,' she replied in her exaggerated, clipped accent. 'I was thinking of you earlier. I just picked up a *gorgeous* GG Marmont Matelassé mini bag. You would love it! It would go great with your lovely leather jacket.'

'Oh, wow! Maybe I could come round and look? My car is in the garage though, so I might be a while since I'll need to take the bus.' I dropped my bait.

'The bus? Oh gosh, no, I wouldn't dream of it. Borrow the Audi. And next time you have an issue you must use my garage, dear. They always give you a courtesy car. I'm getting my nails done this morning, but I'll come by and pick you up at lunchtime and you can drive the Audi back home.'

'Oh, that would be great!' I feigned surprise. 'Thanks so much, Barb.'

'What's wrong with the car, anyway? Actually, don't bother telling me, I won't remember. Just whether it is serious?'

'Oh no, it's only in the garage until tomorrow. I'm not sure what they said. It won't take too long or cost much, so I'm happy.'

'Ah. Well, that's good. Still, it's too long to go without a car. I'll see you at lunchtime!' She hung up the phone. I smiled, I could predict Barb's actions perfectly.

I busied myself with looking presentable while I waited for Barb. My pale face or barely brushed hair wouldn't do. I applied a full face of makeup and curled my hair. For most of my youth I wore it blonde, and only gave in to my natural red after Ben disappeared. Maybe it was time for a change. Although I loved the red, it made me easier to spot in a crowd.

When I looked more like myself, I moved my car into a small car park around the corner where Barb wouldn't see it. Adrenaline kept the fear at bay. The darkness was lurking just out of sight, but it didn't make itself known. Not yet.

Barb arrived at lunchtime just like she'd promised, to my surprise. Barb was an hour late to her own wedding. There was no dramatic reason. She just wanted more time with her bridesmaids. Not that her husband was still around. A car crash had taken his life fifteen years ago. He'd owned a local company which Barb sold for a lot of money after his death. Her deep blue Maserati Quattroporte glinted even in the weak November sun. It was the most comfortable car I'd ever had the pleasure of being a passenger in. I slid into the front seat, feeling like a movie star.

'Hello darling,' she smiled over at me, baring bright white teeth.

'Hi,' I smiled back, showing my own white teeth. I'd always been a little embarrassed about my teeth after not looking after them as a child. I had other things on my mind back then. As soon as I had enough money to be frivolous, I'd asked Barb where she had her teeth whitened.

'How is my sweet little Harry?' She shifted into gear and pulled off from my street.

'Not so little.' I laughed. 'Or sweet. He's acting like a teenager.'

'Oh dear! I suppose it's inevitable,' she said with a grin.

We made small talk all the way to her house. I kept it together, despite wanting to blurt out the plan to her. She was the closest thing I had to a proper mother. But I knew Barb. She would make me go to the police. And other than Swanson, the police were the last thing I needed.

It took less than ten minutes to reach the leafy village of Darley Abbey, where Barb's grand home sat on the outskirts of the abbey itself. She reversed into the driveway as she chatted about what she'd bought for Christmas and who she had left to buy for. She had a lot of friends. Certainly more than I would ever want or need. A few minutes later, I had the key to the Audi in my hand.

'Thanks so much, Barb. I owe you one.' I smiled. Though we both knew there was nothing she would ever need from me.

'You're welcome. Anytime. You know that, don't you?'

'Yes, of course.' The worried look in her eyes aroused my suspicion that Alex had told her something. 'Barb, do you ever speak to Alex?'

'Oh.' She crumpled her brow. 'Not recently, no. He's a detective now, you know.'

I nodded, happy she was telling the truth. 'I just wondered how he was doing.'

'Fine, as far as I know. Sandra told me he's been seeing someone.' She waved a manicured hand around as she spoke.

Despite how long it had been since Alex and I were romantic, a pang of jealousy stabbed at my stomach. 'Who's Sandra?' I tried not to let my disappointment show.

'My sister. Alex's mother.'

The thought of Alex having a mother threw me for a moment. He'd never spoken of her, only his Aunt Barb. The only reason I knew Barb was because she had a spare house when Harry and I needed a new home.

'Are you OK, dear?'

'I just didn't realise he had a mother.' I laughed as soon as the words were out. It sounded ridiculous.

'Oh, yes! Sandra and I don't speak much, mind you. Alex gets his broody ways from her, shall we say? They don't speak much either.' She winked at me.

I smiled and thanked her for the car, then drove back home. I parked across the street and jumped into the back seat where the windows were tinted and I would go unseen to passers-by.

Alex crossed my mind again as I sat there. If he *was* seeing someone, it would explain why he was so off with me earlier. He risked his career for me all those years ago, and now he wanted to forget all about me. Maybe it was for the best. The last thing I wanted to do was get him in any trouble.

It was only early in the afternoon, yet I didn't want to get out of the car and risk the man seeing that I was in the Audi. So I'd stuck some cans of pop and snacks in my handbag so I could eat while I waited. I'd also put in my phone charger, though I could see now that Barb's car had wireless charging installed.

Patience wasn't usually my strong point, but I would have sat there all night if that was what it took. All I needed to do was wait.

The only problem with sitting still was that the Arracht liked to visit when I wasn't preoccupied. Sometimes I didn't mind. He kept me safe, afterall. At other times — when I needed to focus — he drowned out the light too much for me to do so. I was still in control as long as he didn't completely take over my sight. Whenever the corners of my vision darkened, I flicked the band on my wrist and focused on the house. It was difficult, but it worked.

People came and went, walking down the street past my

house. My heart stopped each time I saw a man I didn't recognise. Nerves flew around in my gut, making me nauseous. The darkness fell by 5 p.m. with it being so close to winter.

It was barely 6 p.m. when I watched a tall figure emerge from the right-hand side of the street. I didn't take too much notice at first. Then he caught my eye as there was something familiar about him. He sauntered towards my house on long gangly legs. I strained my neck to see his face, but his hood half-hid it.

I had left the gate unlocked and partially open. He stopped as he reached my front gate, and looked around.

As he turned, he looked straight at the Audi. I thought he'd seen me in the back, but the tinted windows were too dark in the evening gloom. I shifted in my seat, leaning towards the dark glass to get a better view. As he turned to walk into my front garden, his hood shifted to reveal his face.

A familiar face.

A face I once loved.

I stared into the face of Benjamin Bates.

All the air rushed from my lungs at the sight of him. I fumbled with the car door trying to get out to reach him, forgetting I'd locked it. It took a couple of tries to pull the lock and push the car door open. My legs were heavy as I stumbled over the road.

My driveway was short, and by the time I reached the gate, Ben was nearly at my front door. I tried to call out but my voice sounded strange and breathless.

He turned just as the motion sensor lights illuminated the garden. We stood only a few feet away from each other for the first time in eleven years. I expected elation. Yet I stumbled backwards, fighting the sudden urge to run from him.

The sensor light bathed his face in a yellow glow.

As I stepped closer I realised that, although I saw Ben's gangly legs, oval face and strong nose, he looked younger than I remembered. His eyebrows were more prominent, and his nose hooked.

'Kai?' I asked, my voice a whisper.

He ran towards me.

I was too shocked to move.

He was fast. I raised my hands to my face to protect myself. His hands were on me in an instant. I felt his anger as he pushed himself into me with all his might. My head smashed against the ground as I fell, and pain shot through the back of my skull. I kept my hands raised and waited for the attack.

All I could think about was Harry. *Please let me survive for Harry.*

Swanson

Swanson sat back at his desk, once again surrounded by a crowd of other officers. His mobile vibrated in his hand, and an unknown number flashed up. It better be someone with good news. He swivelled around in his chair to face the wall and put a finger in one ear before answering.

'DI Swanson,' he said.

'Alex, it's me.' He knew her flustered voice straight away this time. *For fuck's sake.*

'I told you not to call me.' His voice was as calm as he could make it. Sophie's presence in his life only meant one thing for him: trouble.

'Alex, please, I'm desperate. Kai's just been around my house. I saw him this time. I was watching from a car across the street. He knows where I live. I need to move. I need help.'

'What, like a stakeout? And who the hell is Kai?' He was losing his calm edge. Damn headache.

'Ben's oldest son. He thinks I murdered Ben, like they all do. And now he knows where I live. Even if he does nothing violent, he will at least tell the others where I am. Please, Alex. I don't know what to do. It will take time to move, at least a few days. I just want to make sure Harry is safe until then.' Her voice shook.

'What makes you think he would hurt you or Harry? You don't know if he thinks you're a murderer.' Swanson thought about how he would feel if he believed Sophie had murdered his dad.

He decided Sophie had good reason to be worried.

'It must have been him in my garden before. Tonight I caught him about to break into the house. When he saw me, he pushed me to the ground and ran. He'll be back. I don't think he would hurt Harry, but if he thinks I murdered his dad, why would he *not* hurt me?'

'Fine, text me his full name and everything you know about him, and I'll check him out. That's all I'm doing, Sophie. Then we're done.'

He swivelled back around and threw the phone down on the desk. It landed with a thump.

Bloody Benjamin Bates. He'd always known that case would come back to haunt him.

Swanson didn't get scared often. Fear wasn't useful in any situation. Adrenaline was far better. But Benjamin Bates was not a case he wanted anyone else to look into.

He felt a shadow hanging over him, but didn't move. Maybe if he kept his head in his hands they would disappear. A faint whiff of flowery perfume hit his senses.

'Yes, Hart?' He still didn't look up.

'Stop being an arse. We've got a lead, come on.' DI Hart slapped his shoulder. Her perfectly manicured fingernails scratched his neck.

'Watch your claws.' He raised his head to give her an annoyed look. 'What lead?'

'Remember the second victim said the rapist smelled of petrol? Then the third victim said he smelled of paint?' She

83

grinned like a maniac, the bright red lipstick making her look far too happy for the subject matter.

'Yes?' Swanson wished she'd get to the point.

'Well, we thought that might mean he was a painter, or worked in a paint factory or something, right?'

'Uh huh.'

'Well, there's that massive car manufacturer like five minutes outside of the city, isn't there?' She perched on his desk and held her hand out in front of him, inviting a high five for her big revelation.

Swanson thought out loud. 'So... someone who works in multiple departments. Therefore, someone experienced, someone who knows what they're doing, and has been there a long time. It's a possibility.'

Hart lowered her hand. 'A strong one, right? Well, I mean, maybe not *strong*. I know it's still a long shot. But we have nothing else at the minute. Come on. Let's go because they're open until 8 p.m and for fuck's sake take some paracetamol. I'm sick of that miserable look on your face.'

She rummaged into the depths of her faux leather handbag and, eventually, threw a box of pills at him. How the hell do women fit so much stuff into such small handbags? He ignored the pills, downed the glass of water in front of him, and grabbed his suit jacket from the back of his chair. 'Come on then, Robin.'

'You better stop with that Batman stuff or I'll report you to HR for bullying.' She backhanded his chest hard, making him grunt and laugh. 'So that's what it takes to get you to smile, is it? A slap? I'll remember that. Come on, let's go find this bastard. I've got a good feeling about this.'

'You always say that,' Swanson said as they left the office and entered the claustrophobic corridor that led to the back exit.

'Well, one of us has to be positive, Krypto.'

'Krypto?'

'Superman's loyal dog,' she gave him a sideways glance and smirked.

Swanson drove. It didn't take long to reach the car manufacturer. Although the vast area it covered was like a maze to anyone who didn't work there. They found the reception eventually and walked in to face two young receptionists staring at them with big smiles and white teeth. They were both impeccably dressed, with no blonde hairs out of place.

'Good evening. How can I help?' said the one on the right. She looked at them, her head cocked to one side.

'Evening.' Swanson walked forward. He introduced himself and Hart and showed her his ID. Her smile never faltered. 'We need to speak to someone in charge, please.'

'Sure, I'll be back shortly. Please take a seat.' She stood and gestured to the group of grey, egg-shaped chairs behind them. He smiled but didn't move, and watched her walk away. He took a few steps back to stand with Hart.

'I'm not going to fit in one of those fucking chairs,' he whispered.

She grinned back at him.

A few minutes later, the receptionist returned with a stocky man. He introduced himself as Gary in a thick Derbyshire accent. He gestured for them to follow him through to his office.

Gary, in Swanson's opinion, was a bit of an arsehole. He was grey-haired, short and plump. But he walked with the confidence of someone who was used to people moving out of his way, and he *expected* it to happen. He talked a lot as he led them to a plain office just big enough for a desk, with chairs either side. Swanson and Hart sat and explained to him they were looking for someone.

'So you can't tell me what this bloke has done?' His cocky look changed to one of bemusement. He seemed to enjoy having their attention. They were a new audience for him to show off to. He was clearly not pleased that they wouldn't give him the full story.

'We're just following a line of enquiries, that's all,' Swanson said, using his calm interview voice. He'd dealt with a lot of Garys before. 'There isn't much to say yet. When we know more we'll let you know. If it's pertinent, of course.'

'Of course,' Gary nodded. 'But there really isn't anything I can think to tell you at this stage. There are over a thousand people who work here. We have many tall, white men with facial hair. No one stands out.'

'The man we're looking for also has an accent, though it couldn't be placed. Possibly Russian or French,' Hart said.

'Well, I mean, that doesn't help much if I'm honest. A lot of those white men I mentioned have an accent.'

'OK. Could you possibly get us a list of white men over six feet tall who started working here in the last six months and have an accent?' Hart asked.

'Er, I suppose so. That narrows it down. I'll still need some time.'

Swanson and Hart said their goodbyes to Gary and made their way back to Swanson's car.

Hart waited until they were in the car before voicing her opinion. 'I still feel like this is a lead somehow.' She tugged on the sleeve of her suit jacket.

'Yeah, maybe,' Swanson said, 'I guess we'll wait and see.'

'You don't agree with me,' Hart stated.

'Maybe.'

She turned to look at him as he began driving. 'Well, what ideas have you got?'

'It's nearly 8 p.m. I'll drop you at the office then go back to mine. I have an idea in the making, OK?' He stopped at a red light and gave her a sideways glance.

'Such a team player, Swanson.'

'I know, it's my greatest skill.'

Sophie - January 2008

Ben towered over Sophie as she perched on the sofa. She didn't know what to do. Tears threatened to fall. She choked them back. Crying would make things worse but tears blurred the edges of her vision, anyway. She could see two Bens floating in front of her. She didn't blink. It was easier when he was blurry.

This Ben was a different person entirely. Not *her* Ben. Her Ben would never get this angry. Only fuzzy, double Ben did sometimes.

'Do you promise?' he asked her.

'Mel's my best mate, babe. I don't really have anyone else,' said Sophie. Her voice shook thanks to the stupid lump in her throat.

'You've got me!' he raised his voice. 'Don't I give you everything you need?

'Yes! Of course you do.'

'So what do you need her for?'

Sophie said nothing. She wiped her eyes with the back of her fist.

'Who gave you a home, and food?'

She sniffed. 'You.'

He smiled now. His voice calmed. 'Who got you off drugs?'

'You.'

He broadened his shoulders, seeming larger than usual. 'Exactly. I saved you. So you agree? I give you everything you need?'

Sophie nodded, though she had a sinking feeling in her stomach as if she was walking into a trap.

'Then why would you insult me and everything I've done for you by spending time with someone who is bad for you? Hey?'

She swallowed the bile gathering in the back of her throat.

'How could you throw it all back in my face like that?'

Sophie lowered her head and blinked once. She stared at the floor until her vision blurred again before returning her gaze to Ben. She knew that if she could hold her eyes open, the edges of her vision would go black, like a shadow creeping over anything she didn't want to see. Just like it did when her mum got mad when she was little.

'You're right. She was bad for me before, but I won't touch drugs, babe. It's just nice to have a girl to talk to. We can both have friends.' She tried smiling at him. Her vision was so blurry she couldn't tell if it had any effect on his anger.

'I don't need anybody else, and I thought you felt the same way. We've been together for an entire year. Am I still not enough for you?' He was quieter then, and guilt tugged on Sophie's conscience. The angst in his voice broke her heart, and she hated herself for causing him pain.

'It's just different, you know, girl talk,' she tried to explain, 'I can't talk to you about makeup and hair dye. Or periods!' She chuckled quietly, desperate to lighten the mood.

'You think this is funny?' He didn't raise his voice, but there was a threatening edge to his calmness.

'What? No! Of course not. I'm sorry, Ben. Really, it isn't funny. I was just trying to explain…'

He bent down, his nose an inch from hers. 'Are you going to stop talking to that bitch or not?' He clenched both fists at his side.

Sophie's breath stuck in her throat. She'd never seen him this angry. 'OK, I won't talk to Mel anymore.' She allowed the darkness to take over her vision. She couldn't see Ben at all now. 'Anything for you, babe.'

Before she could duck out of the way, he grabbed a fistful of hair to yank her head back and kissed her hard on the lips. He pushed her onto the sofa and pulled up her dress with his free hand. Sophie kissed him back and closed her eyes. It would be over soon, and he would be her Ben again. All she had to do was lie back, keep her vision dark and make the right noises. Everything would be fine.

Astrid

I walked the fifteen steps from the back door to the front door, back and forth between them. The shadow followed me, always close by. Every time I checked each door handle three times, and each time it was locked, of course. It was a pointless waste of time. But walking back and forth kept the anxiety flowing around my body as I walked, rather than it building up if I sat in one place.

I stopped in the kitchen after I lost track of time, and noticed the pretty bottle of Isle of Wight gin on the counter. Grabbing a gin glass, I poured myself a double serving and perched on the edge of the sofa in the living room.

Alex was going to search for Kai. I just needed to wait for him to call me.

I doubted Kai would come back tonight. He must have waited until he thought I was out, when my car wasn't parked in the drive.

I held the citrus gin on my tongue for a moment before swallowing, concentrating on every sip. After a few minutes my hands no longer shook, and my mind was calmer.

I thought about the situation. Kai could have hurt me if he wanted to. He had the perfect opportunity while I lay helpless on the ground, too shocked to move. Instead, he ran off as quickly as he could. Did he intend to push me, or was it a mistake? I saw his eyes as he ran towards me, wide and fearful. I supposed standing in front of a murderer would scare me, too.

I'd expected to feel elation if I ever saw Ben again. Yet, terror overcame me when I thought he was standing in front of me. The worst part was the relief when I realised it *wasn't* Ben. Maybe it was a relief that it wasn't a stranger, though Kai was little more to me than that, really.

The gin numbed my tired body. I lay down on the sofa and pulled a thin blanket over me, listening to the silence for any signs of Kai trying to break in. I closed my eyes, just for a moment.

It didn't take long for the Moralia to come. *Click, click, click.* My eyes flew open, and a dark shadow scuttled across the floor of the living room. It was as quick as a spider and moved in the same directionless way. *Click, click, click.* I felt invisible hands all over my body, weighing me down. I saw a flash of movement again, and a lump appeared under the blanket by my feet. It moved up, stopping at my knees, then my hips. It clicked every time it stopped.

As it reached my breasts, I felt its weight on my chest: it climbed onto my body. I couldn't breathe. There was a sharpness against my chest. Claws tore at my skin. Silent tears ran down my face. The pain intensified. My body jerked backwards as I fought the force holding me down, but I couldn't free myself from its claws.

It ripped more flesh from my chest and I could no longer bear the pain. As the world turned to darkness, I finally screamed.

I rolled off the sofa and my face smashed against the hardwood floor. More pain shot through my nose and lip.

I ignored it. I got to my feet and stumbled as I ran to the other side of the room to flick on the light. My hands rubbed my chest. There was nothing there. No blood. No gaping hole from the Moralia's claws or teeth. I heaved deep breaths and let the tears come. The blanket had fallen off the sofa with me and lay crumpled on the floor, empty. The Moralia was gone.

I flicked the band on my wrist and closed my eyes, but the panic would not fall away. The pain of the band barely reached me. I ran to check the back door, pulling the handle three times. Then the front door, the back door, the front door. I don't know how long I ran between them, my breath ragged in my throat. Eventually I calmed enough to collapse at the kitchen table in tears. I needed a coffee. A soothing hot coffee always helped.

But by the time I'd made a coffee, daylight had forced its way through the kitchen window. My head ached. I loved waking to natural sunlight on my face, but that morning the powerful light was unwelcome. It was also a signal that it must be nearly 8 a.m.

I jumped up from the kitchen table, spilling my coffee in my rush upstairs to get Harry ready for school.

He didn't respond to my knock.

I opened his bedroom door and his empty bed confronted me. A fear far worse than the Moralia gripped every inch of me.

'Harry!' I yelled. There was no response. Where the hell was he?

I fell to the floor and tried to catch the vague memories of the previous day. My thoughts were like jigsaw pieces which didn't fit together. I clamped my eyes shut. Did I pick him up from school? No.

Was he at a friend's house? Pieces of our conversation came back to me. I scrolled through my phone to check the last texts we sent to each other; he was at the twins' house. Relief flooded through me.

But I had to get a grip. I needed to go for a run. It was the only thing that didn't fail me when the darkness caught up. I threw on some exercise gear, I tucked my phone and key into the phone holder and ran straight out into the morning air. Everything was going to be OK.

Swanson

wanson drove to the hotel first thing the next morning, hoping a young lad like Kai wouldn't be awake and checked out of his room by 7 a.m.

It hadn't been difficult to find Kai. All he had to do was call some local hotels last night. Derby was a small city with only a few main hotels. Swanson found him on the third call, at a hotel chain in the city centre.

The hard part was getting away from the team in the middle of the biggest serial rapist investigation Derby had ever seen, though Hart had finally given him some peace once he said he had an idea brewing. His best ideas always came to him when he was surrounded by silence and his own company. Swanson had pored over all the facts again last night and came up with nothing. The press team had released the facial composite and leads were being collated. A special team had been set up specifically to review the leads and put them into an order of urgency. Hart would let him know when they got something to investigate, which probably wouldn't take too long.

Swanson pulled his suit jacket tighter around his chest to ward off the cold air as he crossed the car park. The purpose-built hotel loomed over the east side of the city, with over two hundred rooms. Inside, the reception area was bright and modern, and far too purple. A well-groomed man stood behind the counter with a broad smile on his face. A handful of guests wandered to and from the breakfast area, but none waited at the counter other than the receptionist.

'Welcome, Sir. Are you here to check in?' Mr Well-groomed asked as Swanson strode up to the desk.

'No. I'm Detective Inspector Alex Swanson.' He flashed his ID. The man's smile faltered as he looked at it, and then back up at Swanson. 'I'm here to see a guest of yours and I need the room number.'

'Oh, erm... OK.' He looked around, spluttering. 'Sure, I think that's alright. What's the guest's name?'

'It is OK. The man's name is Kai Bates.' The ease of the conversation surprised Swanson. There was normally at least a little questioning on whether they could just give him a customer's details. But the man sat down and typed into his computer with no further hesitation. He threw a few nervous glances at Swanson as he searched.

'Kai Bates. Room one-thirty-eight.' He smiled again, bigger than ever.

'Which is where?' asked Swanson.

'Oh, sorry!' the man laughed. 'Up those stairs there, and turn left.'

'Thank you.' Swanson could feel the receptionist's eyes on him as he walked away toward room one-thirty-eight.

It wasn't hard to find. He knocked loudly three times, then heard a mumbling noise and a thud. At least someone was inside.

'Who is it?' a deep voice called.

'Room service,' Swanson shouted back.

More fumbling noises and the door finally opened to reveal

a shirtless, skinny young man yawning and running his hands through dark hair. 'Young man' was right: his face showed too much bum fluff for him to be considered a man yet. Three ugly tattoos marked various places on his chest, and even worse ones covered each arm.

'Hi, sorry for the disturbance and the joke. I'm obviously not room service. I'm Detective Inspector Alex Swanson.' He flashed his ID again. The man's eyes widened. 'I'm looking for Kai Bates?'

'Who is it, Kai?' a woman's voice called out.

Swanson looked over Kai's shoulder. A young woman lay in the bed, facing away.

'Nobody, babe,' he called back.

Swanson raised an eyebrow.

Kai moved into the corridor and pulled the door closed behind him.

'Great, so you are Kai Bates then.'

'I ain't done nothing wrong.' The words rushed out as if he'd said them a million times before.

'OK. That's good to know.' Swanson smiled and leant back against the wall. 'So, Kai. What are you doing in Derby?'

'Visiting a friend.'

'Oh!' Swanson feigned surprise. 'A friend you couldn't stay with because...?'

Kai's mouth opened, then closed again. He shrugged. 'Don't see how that's anyone's business but mine.'

'No... maybe not. Do you know where Rose Way is, by the way?' Swanson raised an eyebrow.

'What about it?'

'Do you know where it is?' Swanson said again.

'Nope.' Kai didn't miss a beat.

'Oh, that was a fast answer. Don't need to think about it for a second? Rose Way?'

'Nope.' Kai shook his head.

'Well, there's been a report of you attempting to break into a house there last night.' Swanson lay out the details with care, revealing as little as possible.

'She's lying!' Kai raised his voice. He was becoming more on edge by the second.

'OK. No need to shout. You clearly don't want your friend in there to know I'm here and that's fine. Keep your voice down, and maybe she won't find out. You said "she's lying"? Who is "she", exactly?'

'Whoever reported that I broke into their house.' His voice quietened to a loud whisper, but he still waved his arms around in frustration.

Swanson got the feeling that Kai was one of those people who was always loud, no matter how hard they tried to whisper. 'I didn't say a "she" was involved, Kai.' Swanson was enjoying himself.

Another look of panic crossed Kai's face. He was an easy nut to crack.

'I didn't say "she", I said "they",' Kai said.

'No Kai, you said "she". And by "she", I assume you mean the lady who lives there. The same lady who supposedly killed your father, right? The one you've been sending notes to and calling in the middle of the night?'

From the expression on Kai's face, Swanson was suddenly unsure.

'Notes?' Kai had already proved he wasn't a good liar, and now he appeared genuinely confused.

'Yes, notes. Phone calls. Breaking and entering. Threatening behaviour,' Swanson said.

'I haven't threatened no one. All I did was push her out of the way! If I'd wanted to hurt her I could have done it. It was dark, and no one was around. But I just wanted to see my brother, Harry. There's no harm in visiting a relative.' Kai smiled in triumph and reached into his pocket. 'I don't even have her phone number. You can check my phone actually.'

'So, you expect me to believe that you didn't send a kid to put a note through her letterbox?' Swanson tried again.

'What kid? I don't have any kids. And I definitely don't know any kids around here, other than Harry. Well, I don't even know him,' he shrugged. 'I just wanted to see Harry to make sure he's OK. Dad would have wanted me to make sure. I've never been to her house before yesterday.'

'Tell me then, Kai. How do you know where they live?'

Kai leaned against the door, folded his arms, and clamped his lips shut.

'Kai, I need to make sure she's safe. Harry too. I need to know how you found them. I need to know who else knows where they are. If you really didn't put the note through their door, then tell me so the police can keep them safe, because someone is threatening them. If it isn't you, then who is it?'

Kai sighed and uncrossed his arms. 'I got a note, too. They pushed it through my mum's door at home. I dunno who it was from.'

'You got a note too? What did it say?'

'Yeah, it was weird, to be honest. Here, I've got it with me.' Kai disappeared into the hotel room and came out less than a minute later. He handed a crumpled piece of paper to Swanson.

'*Murderer, murderer, lies in wait,*

Murderer, murderer, has your brother,
Murderer, murderer, take her fate,
Murderer, murderer, blow her cover.'

'Is she a murderer?' Swanson looked at Kai.

'We found no body. But if you ask anyone round my way, they'll tell you she murdered him,' Kai was strangely calm. No one would guess he was talking about his dad's murder.

'This doesn't tell you the address?' Swanson held the note up between them.

Kai grinned. 'Turn it over, *detective*. It's on the back.' His grin dropped when he saw the look on Swanson's face. 'Look, I've done nothing, OK? I got the note, I drove up, booked into a hotel, and yeah, I panicked when I went round and saw her. Then I went to the pub, met... her.' He jerked his head towards the door. 'And we had sex all night. That's all that happened.'

'OK. How long are you in town for?' Swanson's headache had returned with a vengeance.

'I dunno.' Kai shrugged and looked away.

'Well, for now, stay here. If you need to go home, call this number.' Swanson handed him his own card. He didn't want Kai ringing the station. 'What's your vehicle registration?'

'I don't see why you need that. I just told you I've done nothing wrong.' Kai was getting animated again, throwing his hands around like a stroppy teenager.

'Kai, just make it easy on yourself and tell me.'

'Fine.' Kai muttered his registration plate, went back inside his hotel room and slammed the door without a goodbye.

Swanson cursed, trust Sophie to drag him into a messy situation at the worst possible time. He turned to walk back to the reception. It was even quieter now that the guests were seated for breakfast in the restaurant. As he walked through the exit, Swanson bumped straight into Mr Well-groomed receptionist.

'Oh, sorry, sir!' The receptionist jumped backwards as if Swanson had given him an electric shock, then looked down at the floor. 'Actually, I'm glad I ran into you.'

'You are?' Swanson resisted the urge to tell him to fuck off. He didn't have time for random issues.

'I don't have to provide my name, do I? If I give information?' He looked back up at Swanson, and pulled at the collar of his shirt.

Swanson eyed the receptionist's name tag. James Farrow. 'No. What would you like to tell me?'

'It's about that man on the TV who hurt all those women.' The man fiddled with his hands and continued to look down.

'Oh?' Swanson's interest piqued.

James motioned for Swanson to follow him, and they walked outside together. There was no one around, and James continued to grin as though he was having a normal goodbye chat with a guest. They strolled over to the empty smoking area.

James looked over his shoulder. 'I know a guy fitting the description I heard on the news last night. He stays here sometimes. He's... rough. And he always brings a different woman with him. I think they're prostitutes. Anyway, we got a noise complaint last time and security said there were some weird things going on in the room when the man opened the door.'

'Weird things? Can you elaborate, please?'

'He tried to block the security guy's view, but he'd already seen the girl's arms tied above her head to the bedpost. We see a lot of strange things. The guard assumed it was consensual and did nothing about it. He saw her leave an hour later, and said she looked fine. But when I saw the image last night... well, it looks a lot like him.'

'OK, please get me his name, address, etc. We'll look into it.'

'OK. Give me five minutes.' James's nerves had disappeared, replaced by a giddy excitement that Swanson had seen a thousand times before, though it didn't get any less annoying. James rushed back into the hotel and returned within a few minutes carrying a piece of paper.

'Is there a reward?' James asked.

'Not for anonymous tips. Thank you, Sir,' Swanson said before turning to walk back to his car.

Swanson drove back to his office through the usual rush hour jams. Luckily, he was in no hurry. It was only 7:45 a.m. and he didn't need to be in until the 9 a.m. briefing about the rapist following the press release.

He knew what the briefing was about already. They finally had DNA from the latest victim. He passed the information from James Farrow onto the newly formed team to process and add to the other tips. Looking at everything they had collected so far, it would be a long day but the DNA gave him hope. Maybe, once examined, it would link to someone who was sitting at home waiting to be arrested and it would all be over. A man can always dream.

Astrid

I ran until my legs were so heavy I could barely lift them, and then I ran all the way home. I pushed through the pain with every step, fighting for breath and thinking of nothing other than my aching chest. The fear Arracht didn't leave me, it was a constant shadow on my back.

It was mid-morning by the time I reached home, and my mind was calmer. I was capable of straight thought again, and that was all I needed. If I could think my way out of this, then the Moralia would leave me alone, as long as I could stay calm. I stopped in my front garden, bent over and gasping for breath. Sweat dripped from every pore, but the cool breeze felt amazing against my skin. I wasn't ready to enter the warmth of the house, so I pulled out my phone to text Harry. The voicemail icon flashed up.

'Hi, it's Swanson. Kai got a note, too. It had your address. Call me.'

I tutted loudly at his message. It was as short and sweet as ever. When it came to information, Swanson was a taker and not a giver. Which was the opposite of how he was in the bedroom.

So Kai said he got a note too… that didn't mean anything. What if he was lying? The only thing that made me think it might be true was that I couldn't imagine Kai writing poems to threaten me. I didn't know him well these days, but if he was anything like either of his parents, there is no way he would act that way. His mum has no brains at all, and as much as I loved Ben, poetry and threats were not his style. He was brutally honest. It was one reason I loved him so much. I'd always hated confrontation as a teen, though I had changed a lot since then.

If Kai was telling the truth, then the person writing these threats knew both Kai's address and mine, and also knew how Kai and I were connected. I needed to know what his note said.

I dialled Alex's number. He didn't answer. I fiddled with the phone holder, grabbed the key to unlock my front door, and shoved it inside the lock.

Yet the key wouldn't turn.

I pushed down the handle, and my new calmness disappeared. The door opened easily.

I hadn't locked it. I'd been too preoccupied with getting out for a run.

I edged the door open.

'Hello?' I called out and took one step inside. Silence. I took another step inside, frantically opening up the camera app on my phone to see if anything had happened.

'Close the fucking door, Sophie. Or I'll scream about you murdering my dad so loudly the entire street will hear.' Said a deep voice.

My phone dropped to the floor.

Kai appeared from behind the living room door. *Shit*. He stood still. I swallowed my fear. I could run, but couldn't risk this street thinking I was a murderer. If they called the police, they could take Harry from me. I closed the front door, keeping my face towards him.

'I didn't murder your dad.' My voice shook as I spoke.

'I know.' He still didn't move, though his face softened. 'I just said that so you didn't run. Look, I'm sorry I pushed you yesterday, OK? I just panicked.'

A memory swirled in the back of my mind. Fuzzy thoughts of hands, and pain, and apologies.

'Are you OK?' Kai's voice brought me back to the present.

'Yes. I'm fine,' I snapped. I tried to reach the memory but it had disappeared.

'Can we sit in the living room?' He gestured towards the room behind him.

'I'd rather we didn't.' I stared at him.

'I just want to talk.' Kai looked away. He seemed more sad than angry.

'What about?' I asked.

'My little brother. I have a right to see him.' His face was so solemn. Guilt tugged at me. Maybe Harry had the right to know about Kai, too. I sighed and pointed at the living room.

He walked into the room first, and I waited until he stood at the far side of the room before entering the doorway. There was no way I would trust him because of one measly apology.

He whistled as he reached the far corner of the room and spun around in a slow circle, taking in the expensive decor and large TV.

A mixture of pride and guilt curdled in my stomach. I could have raised Kai here, too.

'Nice place!' he said. His voice was loud, just like Ben's. You'd always hear Ben before you saw him.

'Yes,' I said. There was no point in being modest. 'Harry isn't here.'

'I know. Figured you wouldn't talk to me if he was.'

'I loved your dad.' The words were out before I could stop them, and regret hit me. I didn't want to reminisce. I wanted him to go away.

'I know. I remember.' Kai looked down at his feet.

'What do you remember?' I asked, my curiosity overriding my desire for him to leave.

'When I was a kid, you told me how much you loved him and me. How you wanted me to come and live with you. You never came to get me though.' He raised his head. A small smile lined his face.

'Is that an accusation or a statement?' I couldn't help being defensive. I'd tried so hard to convince Ben to take Kai away so we could raise him together.

'It doesn't matter. My mum needed me anyway so I wouldn't have come.'

I gritted my teeth and fought the urge to say something negative about his mother's parenting skills.

'I just want to see Harry. He's my little brother. He's all I've got left of my dad. Does he even know I exist?'

I shook my head. 'I planned to keep it that way. I thought you all believed I'd murdered Ben. I don't want him getting any thoughts in his head.'

'No. I know you didn't murder him. I believe you,' he paused. 'Harry has a right to know I exist. He has a right to make his own decision about whether to meet me.'

My heart ached looking at his blue eyes. Harry and he looked so alike. They were both the spitting image of Ben. I cleared my throat and looked away.

'I'll think about it.' I stepped away from the living room door

106

to allow him to pass. 'I think you should go now.'

'Fine.' He crossed to the living room door, but stopped when he saw the canvas I used for illustrating.

'What are you doing?' I asked.

He picked up the pencil. 'Giving you my number.' He scribbled something on the paper before leaving the room. He turned to me as he opened the front door. 'But if you don't tell Harry about me, I will.'

'You fucking won't.' I didn't raise my voice. I didn't need to. My intention was obvious. I wasn't letting him near Harry.

'Then I'll be back tomorrow night to tell him myself.' And with that, he closed the door behind him and walked away.

Swanson

Swanson had escaped Hart, and the rest of the team, by hiding in a disused side office that was really more of a storage room these days. He cursed and roughly massaged his forehead with one hand, trying to rub away the painful tension in his brain, as he considered his options. Why did he get involved with Sophie again, when he needed to concentrate on the scumbag getting away with raping women?

He needed to figure out what to do. He'd always known Sophie would need help again one day, and had hoped she wouldn't call *him* when she did. What Swanson really needed was someone to talk it through with, but he couldn't talk to DI Hart this time. She was one of the best detectives he knew, and he didn't need her to figure out the biggest mistake of his career.

There was one person who could help, though. Someone who would understand a fragile mind like Sophie's, and it was the perfect excuse to call. He picked up his mobile and called Summer Thomas. She answered as quickly as she usually did.

'Hey, Summer. It's me.' Swanson cleared his throat and told himself it was a business call, just like any other call he would make for work.

'Hello, DI Swanson.' Her voice was soft, and business-like.

Summer was quietly spoken — the kind of person you can't imagine ever losing their cool. But he knew her words would cut through most people like butter if needed.

'Are you free for some lunch? I could do with your opinion on something. Professionally, of course.' *Shit.* Why had he added that?

There was silence for a moment before Summer answered, 'Yes, OK. If you can meet me close by. Barbara's Baps maybe?'

'Barbar's Baps?' That did not sound like a place he wanted to go.

Summer's soft laugh came down the phone. 'Barbara's! It's just a little cafe round the corner from my flat. They make amazing toasties. Trust me.'

A grin spread across Swanson's face as he hung up, but he made sure he wasn't smiling when he left the oversized cupboard-come-pretend office. He didn't need people asking if he had a lead on the case. He'd barely walked a few feet down the hall when he ran straight into Hart.

'Where the hell have you been?' She eyed him up and down.

'Having some peace and quiet away from you.' He continued down the hall. She rushed after him, her short legs and high heels putting her at a disadvantage.

'You know you love me, really. Where are you going?' She called after him.

'Jesus, you're nosey,' he said.

'Just stop for a sec! Bloody overgrown sunflower.'

'What? Sunflower? Is that an insult, or...?' Swanson stopped and turned to her.

'It was the only tall thing I could think of,' she shrugged. 'Look, Ops ran that information you gave about the hotel guy. He lives half an hour away. They can't get him on the phone.

109

It's a dead line. Someone's gotta chat with him.'

'Why? Did we pull anything relevant? He doesn't work at that car place, does he?' Swanson inwardly cursed Sophie again for dragging him into her mess and preventing him from focusing on the case. He hadn't even looked at the name or address that James Farrow provided.

'The first time he stayed in the hotel was six months ago.' Hart smirked as if she was revealing something massive.

'So?' Swanson wished she'd spit it out.

Hart being Hart, she stood and smirked until it hit him.

'Around the time of the first rape?' he said a second later.

'Yep, and there were similar rapes in his area prior to that...' She tucked her hair behind her ear, a sure sign she was about to launch a full-scale explanation or theory.

'Was there any DNA from those rapes?' he interrupted her.

'Nope.'

'So, I take it you've asked if we can chat to him?' he asked.

Hart nodded.

'When are we going to see him?'

'Once we have the DNA from victim three through, we'll have more to talk about. But we could check him out, at least.'

'OK. Give me one hour.'

He ignored her confused look and stalked off down the corridor and outside to his black Audi. He sped out of the car park and ten minutes later he was sitting in Barbara's Baps waiting for Summer. She'd texted him to say she was running later than expected.

A family sat on the other side of the cafe and four builders sat in front of him. He trusted Summer's cafe choice and ordered two cheese toasties and a jug of water. In fairness, it seemed like the kind of place to not skimp on the cheese.

Summer arrived a few minutes later. She glided into Barbara's Baps in a world of her own, not noticing anything around her, a small smile on her lips. The bell above the door jingled, and all four builders stopped talking for a second to look at her. *Arseholes.* He bit his tongue and stood to welcome her.

Her smile widened when she saw him.

'Hi!' She passed the builders without even glancing in their direction. They quickly turned away and carried on with their conversation.

She took a seat across from Swanson and he sat, too.

'I ordered two cheese toasties in case you wanted one… feel free to order your own thing, though. It's not a problem.'

'Oh! Thanks. That's fine. I often order the cheese toastie here. They're amazing.' She ran her fingers through her hair, getting it out of her face. Swanson pushed away thoughts of his own fingers in her soft hair.

'Great,' He smiled awkwardly and, as if on cue, the greying waitress brought over a toastie each and plopped them down on the table with a smile.

'There you go, ducks. Enjoy.' The waitress trudged back to the counter.

Swanson cleared his throat. Summer didn't hesitate to dive into the toastie. He followed her lead, happy she wasn't shy about her food.

'So,' she said between mouthfuls, 'how can I help the great DI Swanson? God knows I owe you one.'

'You don't owe the police anything. It's my job.' *Fuck's sake.* Why did he act so awkward and stoic around her?

'Fair enough, but I'd like to help if I can?'

'Well, I… we… could use your expertise.' He wished he'd

thought more about how to word his request.

'My expertise?' She looked confused.

'Yes. In mental health,' he explained.

'Oh, I see. Don't you have your own guys for that? I'm not a forensic psychologist until another 18 months of supervision have passed.'

'Yes, I know. We have some experts, but it's rarer than you'd think.'

'OK.' She gave him a look that seemed able to see through any bullshit. 'So, what do you need to know?'

'It's about a little-known case. So this is just between you and me.' He kept his voice low.

'Go on.' She put down her toastie and waved at him to continue.

'On your unit visits, have you ever come across someone who completely forgot committing their crime?'

She furrowed her brow. 'Erm, I've had patients say it. Whether it's true is anyone's guess.'

His voice became more urgent. 'Can it be true, though? Is it possible?'

'Well, yes. It's possible for people to forget traumatic events or black out. It's called dissociative amnesia.'

'Don't people remember eventually?' Swanson asked.

'Often, yes. Not always.'

'Does it cause any further problems?'

'Problems? Mentally?'

Swanson nodded.

'Well, it's not like anterograde amnesia, where the patient suffers an inability to make fresh memories. It's usually retrograde amnesia, so they *can* remember new information and therefore make fresh memories. The majority don't even realise they've had amnesia until someone makes them aware of it. Their brain might even fill in the details with new fake memories. But dissociative amnesia is associated with several things. Personality traits, genetics, previous psychological trauma from a young age and yes, other comorbidities such as personality disorders.'

'Like psychopaths?' Swanson asked.

Summer smiled. 'No. Psychopaths aren't an actual thing. Psychopathy can be a *symptom* of a personality disorder, such as antisocial personality disorder. But that's not related to dissociative amnesia. If a murderer suffers from amnesia it's probably because they're so traumatised by their act that their brain has forgotten it. Unlike your average psychopathic murderer. The dissociative amnesia here would more likely be linked to avoidant or dependent personality disorders or obsessive-compulsive disorder.'

'Hmm. I didn't realise you knew so much,' Swanson said.

'What are you trying to say?' She looked away as she laughed, once to the side and then down to the floor. As if her own laughter embarrassed her.

'Just that I'm impressed.' He smiled, and noticed her cheeks colour.

'Thanks.' She took another bite of her toastie and swallowed. 'I know a lot because of my brother, I suppose.'

'Did you visit him at the hospital address I gave you?' Swanson picked up the last bit of his own toastie. It was as good as Summer said.

'Yes. He isn't there anymore. They wouldn't tell me where he's gone.' She still smiled, but the sadness was clear in her dark eyes. Swanson felt an urge to make it go away.

'Oh, you should've said. I can look into it for you.' The words

113

were out before he considered them. Shit. Another favour amid everything else?

'I didn't want to ask... but I'd be grateful.' She smiled over at him. Fuck it.

'Want to grab a drink later? We can talk some more?' Swanson asked.

She looked at him, her eyes widened. She looked away again before answering. 'I have Joshua tonight. But I'd love to another time.'

'Sure, just let me know. I have to get back to this case now, though.' Swanson felt his own cheeks colour. 'See you.' He stood and rushed out of the cafe before she could say goodbye.

That was the last time he was asking someone out. This lunch had been useful, though. He knew something was off with Sophie, and maybe Summer would help if he did her a favour and found her brother.

Sophie - September 2008

The two-bed semi loomed in front of Sophie. Despite its peeling render and grey window sills, it felt like her own grand castle. Grass tickled her knees as she stood at the bottom of the paved garden path which led to the front door. They would need to buy a lawnmower, and definitely some weedkiller.

It had been over a year since they fell in love, and on their one-year anniversary they had celebrated in the registry office with two of Ben's friends as their witnesses. Mel had refused to come. She didn't think Sophie was good enough for Ben. Now they had their very own home. Not a room in someone else's house or in a tiny flat, but their own house to live in together, alone.

She was Mrs Sophie Bates, and this house was their fortress to keep out any enemies. Though any enemies — or friends — now lived over one hundred and fifty miles away. The rent for a two-bedroom house in Ashfield cost the same as their tiny London flat. Here was somewhere they could *actually* start a family. Here, she would make Ben happy and give him everything he ever wanted.

He squeezed her hand, and she turned to look at him. He was staring at her with a sweet smile on his face.

'Look what I've done for us, babe. Our own home away from all of those arseholes.' He was so proud, and her heart swelled with pride too.

'I'm proud of you, babe,' she said. 'Come on, let's get inside.'

'It's me and you against the world now,' he replied as they walked hand-in-hand up the path.

'Yep. And maybe Kai, one day? He deserves so much better than Emmie as a mother.' Sophie wouldn't give up hope Kai could live with them.

'I've told you like a hundred times he won't be allowed. Emmie won't even let him visit. Best to leave him where he is. She can forget her child support money if she won't let me see him.'

Sophie pushed away the heavy feeling in her heart, and didn't share her thoughts. There was no point annoying him on such an otherwise perfect day. She would convince Emmie to let Kai visit, and she'd make sure he didn't want to return home. She could look after him the way a little boy deserved.

The front door emerged in front of her like a gateway to a calmer world. It was the cleanest part of the house, having recently been kicked in and, therefore, replaced. The owner had mentioned it to Ben during his initial visit the previous month. A domestic dispute, apparently.

'I hope the fella who kicked the door in doesn't think she still lives here,' Sophie said, 'he might come back.'

'Nah. They've locked him up. Besides, there's a cop living next door. I had a chat with him when I came to check the place out last week.' Ben squeezed her hand again. 'And you've got me. Men like that are cowards. They're scared of real men. Even if it *does* turn out to be a dangerous street, plenty of other places are affordable compared to London. I can work

116

anywhere as an electrician.'

'And I can work anywhere as an editor, thanks to you. I still can't believe you paid for the course.'

Ben jangled the keys in front of her, his grin wide, and Sophie laughed as he unlocked the front door. He pushed it open slowly, but as she went to walk in, he stopped her.

'Wait, Mrs Bates!' He picked her up, making her squeal. She wrapped her arms around his neck, and he carried her over the threshold.

'Christ, you're heavier than you look!' He plonked her back down in the hallway.

Sophie looked around the tight space, up at the bare stairs and through the door to the empty living room. Tears stung her eyes, and she sniffed them away.

'What's wrong?'

'I'm just so grateful, Ben. You've got us this house, our jobs... I don't know how to thank you. You're amazing. I don't deserve you.'

'You've got the rest of our lives to make it up to me, Mrs Bates.' He swooped her up into his arms again. 'Starting right now.' He winked and kissed her.

Sophie was more than happy to oblige. She giggled as he carried her to the kitchen and sat her on the table. It was time to start their own family in their perfect new home.

Astrid

I sat on the floor after Kai left, flicking the elastic band on my wrist as the shadow enveloped me. I didn't bother to wipe away the tears. It was soothing to let them fall.

Only one thing could bring me out of the darkness when it was this bad: Harry.

I had to be OK for Harry, and I still needed help to protect him. Alex had helped me enough, so I called Barb instead. I held my breath for a moment to stop the tears and pulled out my phone to call her. She answered almost straight away.

'Hey, Barb. It's Astrid,' I said in the most neutral voice I could manage.

'Yes, darling. Phones do this wonderful thing now where the person's name shows up when they call you,' she said with a chuckle, 'are you OK?'

'Oh, yes.' I laughed too, glad she couldn't see my embarrassed face. 'Are you free? I could do with some company.'

'Sure, do you want me to come over?' Barb said. There was an edge of concern in her voice. Her accent was never as clipped when she was worried or angry.

'No, don't do that. I'll come to you. Be there in an hour?' I tried to make my voice lighter, as though I had no cares and no black shadow following me.

'Yes, perfect. I'll get some drinks ready,' Barb said, her accent sharp again.

I hauled my shaky body off the floor and stood for a moment, letting the blood return to my legs. One step at a time, I fought through the shadowy hallway. I'd kept my sanity together for ten years. I would not lose it now. Though last time I had Alex to help me through.

I flicked on the bathroom light and, to my relief, the shadow reduced to the size of a football. My anxiety eased, and my strength was building. I washed the sweat and tears away in a quick shower and reapplied foundation, blusher, and mascara before tying my hair into a bun. My hands still shook as I spritzed some perfume, but it would have to do.

I checked the back door and every window in the house before I pulled on my boots and left. I had to get out of the car three times in the drizzling rain to check I'd locked the front door. Eventually I drove away.

I reached Barb's house within ten minutes, and checked my face in the front mirror of my car, convinced I would look a mess. It surprised me to see a half-presentable face staring back at me. My boots thudded against the charming woodstone paving that led to her front door, and I used the heavy door knocker to let her know I'd arrived. It took her a minute to answer, but she opened the front door with her usual flourish.

'Oh, Astrid, darling! Come in.' She waved me inside, and I instantly felt calmer. A welcoming aura always surrounded Barb, which made me feel strange... in a good way. It was how I imagined normal people felt when visiting their mother. She didn't look the motherly type, though she had two sons and a grandchild. She wore her grey hair up in a graceful bun and brown Ralph Lauren boots to match a floral ankle-length dress.

I smiled and stepped into the entrance hall. She had decorated the walls in mustard yellow Farrow and Ball paint, which contrasted against a dark oak floor. And hung what I assumed to be *expensive* paintings on the walls.

I followed Barb to the living room, which was just as decadent, with antique hardwood chairs positioned strategically in front of a bookcase that spanned the length of the back wall. A luxurious Chesterfield sofa in the middle of the room stole the limelight. Over the fireplace hung a sizeable canvas picture of Barb, her late husband and their two grown-up sons. Both sons were the image of Barb.

What surprised me, though, was a well-dressed man sitting on the sofa.

'Oh, Charles, meet Astrid.' Barb beamed and walked over to the man.

He stood from the sofa and smiled. He was younger than Barb, maybe mid-forties. I stifled a laugh at Barb's sly wink behind his back and walked over to hold out my hand.

'Lovely to meet you, Astrid,' he said, in an accent almost as clipped as Barb's, though not as realistic. His hands were rough as he took mine and planted a kiss on the back of it. They reminded me of a builder's hands.

'You, too.' I smiled and took my hand away.

'Come on, dear. Let's talk in the garden. I'll put on the heater to keep us warm.' Barb grabbed my other hand and pulled me along like a schoolgirl.

Outside, the drizzle had stopped and the late afternoon sun once again broke through. It was still chilly, and I wrapped my jacket around me as we sat under Barb's gazebo. I hated that designer jackets were never warm enough, but after years of second-hand clothes, I cared more about showing my hard work than being cold. I could handle a few goose pimples.

Barb had already prepared a jug of lemon and water for the table, along with two empty glasses. She poured us a glass each before taking her seat across the table from me.

'So, tell me, Astrid. What's wrong?' She shifted in her seat as if getting comfy for a long conversation.

'Wrong?' I cocked my head to one side and focused on her.

'Yes, you sounded upset earlier.' She raised an eyebrow.

'Oh, sorry. No. Nothing's wrong. Just having an off day. Harry is out at the twins' house. He has been since yesterday. It gets lonely, eventually.' I did my best to throw her off. 'Tell me about Charles. Where did you meet him?' Her face lightened at the mention of Charles.

'Oh, there's nothing going on. We met about a month ago in Waitrose Cafe. It turns out we have quite a lot in common! But he's much too young for me. We went to the museum together this morning. He'll be off soon once he's decided which book to borrow.' She looked wistfully back at the house.

'Oh, I thought you'd met a nice toy boy.' I grinned.

'No, no. I have no interest in toy boys.' She waved her hand at me again. 'Now, Astrid. Tell me what's really bothering you and I'll see what I can do to help.' She shifted her focus back to me and gave me a serious look.

I sighed. I did trust Barb, yet I was unsure where to even start. 'When I came to Derby, what did Alex tell you about my past?'

'He said you had an awful ex-husband and needed a safe place to stay with your boy. That's it really. It was all I needed to hear.' She placed a hand on my knee and squeezed before removing it.

'My husband wasn't awful. But his family was. And when he disappeared they got a lot worse.' I paused. 'Well, Kai, my husband's oldest son, visited me today. He wants to meet Harry.'

Barb didn't exhibit the shock I'd expected. Instead, she leaned back in her chair and gestured theatrically for me to continue.

'The thing is, his family aren't the kind of people I want anywhere near Harry, and Harry doesn't even know Kai exists.'

'Why not?' Barb sat forward and raised an eyebrow.

'They're a hot mess, Barb. Jobless, dirty, mostly drug addicts or alcoholics.'

'Oh dear.' She looked deep in thought for a moment. 'Is there any other reason?'

'Like what?' I eyed her. What did she already know?

'I don't know, darling. It just doesn't seem enough that you'd be so concerned you would call me as soon as you'd seen him.' She waved her arms again.

Barb couldn't sit still... but then it was normal for her to talk with her hands. It didn't necessarily mean she was nervous or hiding anything. There was something off today though, and I couldn't put my finger on what the issue was. The atmosphere in the house was different. The welcoming aura was gone. I studied Barb, and she stared back at me with one eyebrow raised. This was Barb, for God's sake. The only friend I'd had for a decade.

'Well, they think I murdered him,' I said.

Barb shifted in her seat and looked down. She clasped her hands together on her knee, and took a breath before she looked back at me. 'Ah. I see. And did you?'

'Barb!' I stood as though she'd poked me with a hot branding iron.

'Calm down, dear!' She was as calm as ever. 'I have to ask. Sit.'

'I would never hurt somebody I loved.' I sat back down as she asked, though my glare didn't lessen.

'I know. But I don't know if you loved him. He could have deserved it, for all I know.'

'What? No! Like I said, Ben was amazing.' I blinked back more tears.

'Well, why do they think you murdered him? Was there a body?'

'No. He disappeared. His mum and sister think he would never have disappeared without telling them. They think I was some sort of control freak and I kept him from them. We moved away, but that was Ben's idea. When he first disappeared, they hounded me constantly, saying I was covering something up.' The words came out in a rush. I hadn't spoken to anybody about Ben or his family for years.

'And that's why Alex asked if I had a place for you to stay?' she asked.

There was something about her tone that I didn't like. Or was it the atmosphere still bugging me? I looked behind my shoulder at the house, and goose pimples prickled my arms. Coming here was a mistake. 'Look, I have to go.'

'No, wait. You just got here. Talk to me. Maybe I can help.'

I drained my glass of water and stood. 'No. I'm OK, honestly. Sorry for snapping. It's been a long day.'

'Call me when you get home.' She smiled, but her words didn't hold her usual warmth.

'Will do. I'll see myself out.' I walked away as quickly as I could manage and jogged through the house. The living room was empty. Charles was no longer there. I rushed to my car, dropping the keys halfway across the drive. My tyres screeched as I pulled off the drive.

Whatever it was, with Barb acting off and Alex not overly interested, it was up to me to protect Harry from Kai or anyone else that threatened our happiness. I checked my watch. He would finish school in two hours.

I pulled up outside the school to wait for him. I texted Harry and told him I'd be waiting in my car outside the school at pickup time.

I decided on one thing for sure. I had to tell Harry about Kai.

The weirdness with Barb had thrown me even more than Kai's visit. Or maybe the weirdness was *because* Kai's visit affected me so much. Had I caused the weird vibe with Barb? I couldn't tell. I sat in the car and stared at the school gates across the road. I stayed back a little, so I didn't look dodgy to any passers-by.

Knowing Harry was in there calmed me. My Harry. My reason for breathing and living through anything that throws itself at us. It was only a few minutes later when the school called me.

Harry had walked out of maths class an hour ago to use the toilet.

Nobody had seen him since.

Swanson

S wanson rushed back to the office to pick up Hart. She stood outside in the rear car park, waiting for him with a scowl on her face. Though that look was fairly common for her. Swanson was sure she specifically drew her eyebrows to look angry each morning. She had bruised his arm when he said that to her face.

She took a step forward as he slowed the car to a stop next to her. As soon as she opened the car door, she began her rant. 'Where the hell have you been? I've been waiting ages and had Murray in my face—'

'Hart! I had to see a friend. It's sorted now. Stop whining.' He laughed as her fist connected with his arm. 'Ow. You know I'm just winding you up. Tell me what you found out and where we're going then.'

'You're a prat. Look, his name is Peter Johnson. He lives half an hour away, or at least that was the address given to the hotel. His house is in Pinxton.'

'But if he lives in Pinxton, why get a hotel?' Swanson asked. 'That makes no sense. It's only half an hour away.'

'Hmm. Maybe he wanted to lie about where he lived, or have a drink?'

'Maybe, but you'd think he'd go further than thirty minutes

down the road if that was the case.' Swanson pulled onto the A38 to Ashfield and put his foot down.

'Maybe he doesn't drive or have much money, and a hotel ate his travel budget. It is a terrible hotel he chose, so he's probably not rolling in it.' Hart scrunched up her nose, clearly disgusted at the thought of staying in a budget hotel.

'Hey, I always stay in that chain when I'm going away for a night or two.' Swanson gave her a faux hurt look.

'That doesn't surprise me.' She rolled her eyes.

Swanson laughed. 'We'll know more when we see his house.'

They fell quiet while Swanson drove for another fifteen minutes up the A38 and into Pinxton.

Hart fiddled with the in-car satnav and entered the postcode just before the Pinxton junction. Swanson followed the directions through the town and then turned left into a rat run of streets. Wonky gates, wheel-less bikes and gardens filled with rubbish flew by them. Swanson drove close behind a clapped out Fiat, which parked halfway down a small cul-de-sac just before the satnav alerted them that their destination was on the right.

They glanced at each other.

'Lovely,' said Hart, 'a really nice place to bring kids up.'

'Stop being judgemental,' Swanson replied. A teenager across the road spotted them, stuck his middle finger up and legged it. 'Or don't.' He muttered.

They found number eight Willow Gardens near the end of the cul-de-sac, cornered in by four other properties. None appeared to be very well looked-after, and number eight was no exception. There was no driveway. The compact front garden was a mass of knee-high grass and extensive weeds. A few ancient slabs were dotted throughout, and fighting to form some sort of a path to the front door. Swanson pulled up outside the house and the pair got out of the car and stood together, looking up at the house.

Hart sighed. 'Let's get this over with,' she muttered.

The smell of dog shit stung Swanson's nostrils. He held his breath and swung open the garden gate, which creaked in protest. The pair took their time to walk up to the front door, and deliberately stuck to the slabs to avoid any hidden surprises in the grass. Swanson knocked on the door, which shook despite him trying to be gentle.

He stood back to let Hart take centre stage. Men warmed to her more. Well, they did until she opened her mouth.

Footsteps approached, and the shadow of a person got closer through the frosted glass. A large man opened the door and towered over Hart. He looked about sixty, and was holding a yapping Yorkshire Terrier in his arms.

'Peter Johnson?' Hart asked. She had a smile on her face, Swanson noted. It would be the dog. Hart loved dogs.

'Yes?' The man smiled back but looked surprised to see two people in suits who knew his name.

'I'm Detective Inspector Hart, this is my colleague Detective Inspector Swanson.'

The man nodded to her introduction, shushing the terrier. It stopped barking, thankfully. Dogs with small man syndrome were the worst. Swanson didn't understand why anyone would want one.

'We were hoping you could help us with something. Could we come in, please?'

'Oh yes, of course, love. Come in out of the cold.' The man waved them in and the dog growled. 'Don't mind him, I'll put him in the kitchen.'

127

They followed Peter into the tiny hallway and he gestured to the left, telling them to sit on the sofa and that he'd be back in a minute.

The living room was full of pictures of the same five or six people. Family, Swanson assumed. One kid looked familiar, though Swanson couldn't place him. It looked clean but a musty smell hung in the air, like it often did in an older person's, though Peter Johnson wasn't that old really. Hart sat on the beige sofa and glanced around, no doubt taking everything in with her sharp eyes.

Peter returned in less than a minute with a plate of biscuits. 'Here you go.' He smiled at them both, 'Please, take a biscuit. Would you like a cuppa?'

'Oh. No, thank you,' Hart said.

Swanson sat next to her on the sofa. He sank into the old cushions a bit too easily. The weights would have to come back out soon.

Peter took a seat in the armchair opposite them. He moved slowly, as if he was in pain. He didn't look like he could attack anyone. 'How can I help?' he asked.

Hart leaned forward. 'Well, we wanted to ask you about a recent hotel stay—'

'Hotel stay?' Peter interrupted, looking confused.

Swanson thought he'd better say something or he might just look like the muscle. 'Yes, in Derby.'

'Oh dear, I haven't been to Derby in years.' Peter shook his head, 'Sorry, but I don't think I'll be able to help.'

'Oh, right. Only, the hotel gave us your name and address,' Hart said.

'*My* name and address? They must be mistaken, love. I can't travel too far. I'm not in the best of health. My son has to come round most weeks just to check I'm alive.' His chesty chuckle suggested he smoked a pack of cigarettes a day despite his poor health.

'So, you haven't been to Derby at all? Or stayed in any other hotels recently? Say, over the last few months?' Hart tried again.

'No, dear. I wish I had. It would be nice to get away. Even if it's just to little old Derby.'

Swanson and Hart glanced at each other.

'Do you know how the hotel might have gotten your name or address?' Hart asked.

'I have no idea, love. Something to do with them computers maybe?'

'Computers?' She asked.

'Yes, them computer things they use now, the iPods and such. They make a lot of mistakes, don't they?'

'Not this kind of mistake.' Swanson interjected.

'Ooh, well. I really don't know what to say.' The man looked down at the floor, deep in thought, but he said nothing further.

'OK, Sir. Sorry for wasting your time,' Hart said. 'Could you give us a call if you do remember something that might be useful, please?' She stood and stepped closer to Peter.

'Of course, lovey.' Peter took the card Hart handed to him and hauled himself out of his chair to walk them out.

The pair stepped carefully down the driveway again and climbed back into Swanson's car.

'What do you think?' Hart asked him once he'd started the car.

'I don't know, to be honest.' Swanson tried to assess his feelings. He did not get the impression that Peter Johnson could hurt anyone easily. 'He actually seemed to be telling the truth.'

'Yeah, I think so, too. If not, he's one of the best liars I've ever spoken to.' Hart looked out of the window and chewed her lip.

Thirty minutes later they reached the office car park and Swanson pulled up in a space at the back.

'Why do you always have to park at the back?' Hart moaned.

'So you have to walk further.' He replied without missing a beat.

She tutted loudly and opened her door to get out. Swanson grabbed his things to do the same but the phone buzzed as he picked it up.

'You go in, I'll be in soon,' he called after Hart.

She waved a hand, slammed his car door shut and walked off.

Once alone, he unlocked his phone and opened the new text message.

It was from Summer with an address. *Eddie*.

He cursed. Another place he didn't have time to be.

But there was no way he would let her go alone.

Sophie - August 2009

Ben didn't say a word the entire drive home from the hospital, and Sophie didn't dare say anything either. A ball of devastation curled up inside her, one she knew she could never recover from. It would stay there as a shadow on her heart. Just like the last time.

Now, leaning against the kitchen counter for support, she sobbed silently, trying to hide her crying from Ben.

'Look at me,' he said.

She turned to face him but could not stop the tears from flowing this time.

'I'm sorry,' she whispered.

His nostrils flared.

The fear overcame her sadness. She took a deep breath and held it, controlling her sobs. 'I'm sorry, Ben,' she said.

'Sorry?' he whispered, 'that doesn't help. All I've done for you, and you can't give me the one thing I want in return. Maybe I should have listened to Mel. She said you were useless.'

The familiar dread sat in the pit of her stomach as she swallowed back more tears. She never used to upset him this much.

'We can adopt?' She instantly regretted her words. *Why was she so stupid?* They would never allow them to adopt with his criminal record after the fight with Emmie. It didn't matter that it was Emmie who had attacked him. And now, they would suffer because of it.

'Who would let a former drug addict like you adopt a child?' His face turned a pale shade of red and he turned away.

'I... I... don't know. I'm talking rubbish. I'm sorry. I'm upset too.'

His fist connected with her face and pain exploded through Sophie's eye. His hand was around her throat so fast she didn't even see him move.

'*You're* fucking upset? You're a waste of fucking space.' His voice was a low growl.

Sophie's breath stuck in her throat. Her head throbbed. She tried to raise her hands to pull him off her neck, but his body got in the way. The edges of the room turned a fuzzy black as a shadow enveloped her.

Her eyes bulged and, in the shadow oozing across the ceiling, she saw a face. A gaunt face, too decrepit to distinguish as either man or woman. Wisps of dark hair trailed from its head, and she watched in horror as its emaciated body emerged within the shadow. An aged hand reached out to her from the ceiling. Skin had fallen from some fingers to reveal grey bone underneath.

Ben released his grip just enough to allow her to breathe, and leaned his face so close that she could smell cigarettes on his tongue. She took a painful deep breath. The shadow, and the thing within it, disappeared. Had she seen death?

'You will be fucking sorry,' Ben whispered.

He let go of her neck and she breathed deeply again. A second later he grabbed her shoulders and wrenched her around. She stumbled. Ben grabbed her and forced her to stand. He grabbed a fistful of her hair and bent her body over the kitchen counter, pushing her face hard against the ice cold countertop. He reached up her dress and pulled down her underwear.

Horror hit her as she realised he wasn't just going to punch her this time.

'Please, Ben. No,' she tried to say, but her words were mumbled against the countertop pressing against her cheek.

He pressed her head harder into the kitchen unit. She cried out, her ear was being crushed.

'Shut the fuck up. This is the least you owe me,' he growled, 'we're going to do this every day until you get fucking pregnant, you hear me?'

Three loud bangs echoed around them.

Ben let go. Someone was knocking on the door. His eyes were wild with panic.

'Don't move,' he told her, his voice a rushed whisper.

She froze, still bent over the icy counter with her dress above her hips.

The person at the door knocked again, louder this time.

'Fuck's sake, go into the living room.' Ben buttoned up his trousers as Sophie pulled up her underwear and ran into the living room. She knelt on the floor and half-closed the door so she could hide behind it and look through the crack. Her body shook, and she took deep breaths to try and calm herself.

At the front door Ben yelled: 'Who is it?'

'It's me, from next door,' a deep voice called back.

Ben swore under his breath before opening the door and smiling widely.

'Hi. How are you, mate?'

Sophie could only see Ben, but their neighbour's voice was loud and clear. She couldn't remember his name.

'I'm good, thanks. Thought I heard shouting. I wanted to check if everything is OK?' The neighbour took a step inside the hallway.

Ben stepped to the side and blocked the path inside the house. 'We're fine, mate,' Ben said, still smiling. 'What did you hear?'

'Shouting, crying, banging. Is Sophie in?'

'Must have been the telly. She's not in, she's at a mate's. Thought I'd watch a film while she was gone,' Ben shrugged. He was a good liar.

Sophie's heart quickened as she hid behind the door. She could see the man's outline through the crack and felt an urge to reach out to him. But then, what would Ben do? The sweet Ben that she knew and loved? Where would she go without him?

'Oh, great. I thought some arsehole had broken in or something,' their neighbour said.

'Yeah, I bet, mate.' Ben still grinned, yet his eyes were just as crazy as they had been in the kitchen.

'I'd better go.' The man stepped back and disappeared from Sophie's view. They muttered bye to each other, and Ben closed the front door.

Sophie stayed kneeling on the floor, she closed her eyes and waited for Ben to tell her what to do. To her surprise, he said nothing. His footsteps shook the ceiling as he stomped up the stairs. Then she heard their bedroom door shut.

She placed a hand on her chest and breathed. She was safe for now. He would say sorry soon and he would never do it again. There was no way he meant it. It was going to be OK.

The haunting face of the shadow stuck in her mind more so

134

than Ben's attack. What the hell was that thing? Her phone lay on the floor next to her, where it had fallen from her cardigan pocket. She grabbed it and flicked open the browser to look up shadow monsters. Nothing came back at first: some stuff about a TV show, but eventually she saw an image of a starving, barely human creature with rotten skin staring back at her. She gulped, and continued to read.

'A fear Arracht is an abandoned corpse of an emaciated human which signals terror and death. It originates from Irish folklore and roughly translates to fear monster.

It is said that it appears when you feel fear so terrible that it is about to consume you, and it feeds from that fear to survive. When sucking the fear from a person, it will suck the very soul, too.

Leaving nothing but an empty vessel in its place.'

Astrid

I'd barely hung up the phone when I jumped out of my car and ran across the road to the school. The rotund headteacher, Mr Hardiman, stood outside the main entrance. His cherry red face was a deeper shade of red than usual. His mouth opened and closed when he saw me arriving within seconds of our phone call, but he said nothing.

'Where are the twins?' I said between heavy breaths, 'they'll know where he is.'

'They're in a lesson. I spoke to them before calling you. They don't know where he is.' He was far too calm for my liking. I wanted to grab him by the shoulders and shake him. Didn't he realise how serious this was?

'Then let me speak to them,' I demanded.

'I'm sorry, I can't allow it without their parents present.' He shrugged his large shoulders apologetically. 'But come in and we'll talk some more.'

I didn't have time for his bullshit. Before he'd finished his sentence, I'd pulled out my phone and dialled the twins' mum.

'Hi, Betty.' I turned away from the infuriating Mr Hardiman. 'Harry's gone missing.'

'What! No.' Betty gasped. 'What—'

'I need you to come to the school and speak to the twins.

They'll know where he went.'

'Oh, of course! I'll be there in five minutes. Oh, gosh. OK. Five minutes, Astrid. Don't panic.'

I heard her rustling around with a coat as she hung up. I turned back and scowled at Mr Hardiman. His face was getting redder every minute.

'So, explain to me how my child got out of your school?' I asked.

'He went to the toilet in maths class, and he didn't come back.' His voice was weak.

'And no one saw him leave? What about the receptionist?'

'This is a secondary school, Miss Moor. It's a little different to primary. The small gate at the end is always open. Sixth form kids are in and out all day. We trust the kids not to walk out, and... well... they never usually do.'

'You have a duty of care to the children who attend your school. If anything happens to my boy, I will hold you personally responsible.' My panic was building, but I swallowed it down. The shadow was not going to stop me from finding Harry. He was the only thing that kept me sane.

'Why don't we go inside and get some tea? We can talk in my office?' he asked with a smile.

'No. We'll wait right here for Betty.' I was sick of talking to him. I turned away and looked at the gate.

Betty turned up a minute later, running over to me with a young baby in her arms. She was breathless by the time she reached us and was wearing two different shoes.

'Show me where they are,' she demanded.

I liked Betty. She was a *proper* mum. She could sew, bake, and run anywhere with her baby in tow. Even if she didn't realise her shoes did not match. Not like me. I was the type of mum who felt out of her depth, constantly wishing someone more 'adult' was around. I felt a sense of camaraderie as soon as she arrived. She would back me.

'Come to my office and I'll call for them,' smiled Mr Hardiman. Why the hell was he smiling so much? It was getting harder with each passing minute not to punch him in the face.

We strode through the school corridors in silence, passing the odd teacher or child. Most were still in lessons. I hated the smell of schools. It was a sickly combination of sweat, deodorant, cheap food, and disinfectant. And it made me feel sick at the best of times, never mind when I was already so nauseous. It didn't take long to reach the office, and Mr Hardiman's secretary went to collect the twins. Betty and I sat on two hard chairs across from the headteacher's desk. The baby on her lap stared at me with wide eyes.

'Are you OK?' Betty peered at me.

I tried to speak. I tried to say 'yes, I'm OK. I'm sure everything will be fine' but no words came out and tears threatened to fall, so I shrugged instead.

Behind her, the shadow had grown without me even noticing. It had taken over the entire wall. As I watched, the emaciated hand of the Arracht appeared. It was a shock of white against the dark shadow. Pale bones glistened behind dripping flesh.

Something grabbed my leg. I jerked away and looked down.

It was Betty. 'Astrid? Do you need some tea?' she said. Her voice sounded far away.

I shook my head and looked away from the Arracht. There would be no death today.

The twins arrived a few seconds later. The two ginger boys threw each other nervous glances and fiddled with their fingers as their mother tried to coax the truth out of them.

I forced myself to focus, but it was hard as there were so many fragmented possibilities running through my brain. I didn't know which one to focus on. Was Kai responsible for Harry's disappearance? Or someone else? Or was it nothing to do with Ben and related to something else entirely?

'Like I said, boys, you're only in trouble if you *don't* tell me what happened. I don't care what you've done, I only care that Harry is safe,' Betty was saying to them.

I clamped my lips shut and sat on my hands to stop the urge to shake the truth out of the boys.

'He didn't tell us where he was going today!' protested Tom, looking at George for backup. His brother nodded earnestly in agreement.

'Today?' I asked.

The boys' cheeks flushed. They wouldn't meet my eye and looked down at the floor instead.

'He's been gone other days?' I glared at Mr Hardiman, who looked more purple than red now.

The twins' faces dropped as they realised they'd landed their friend in it. 'No!' they said in unison.

'Boys!' said Betty sharply. 'Look at me please.'

The pair kept their heads low but peered up at their mother.

'There's a man he speaks to sometimes. In the gap next to the woods,' said George.

I tasted metallic bile in my mouth as my stomach lurched. 'What did the man look like?' I asked.

The twins shrugged their shoulders. 'We haven't seen him. Harry just told us about him,' said George.

'What did he tell you about him?' their mother asked.

The boys didn't answer, but looked at each other with wide

eyes.

'Boys, if you don't tell me everything right this instant I will throw every goddamn electronic device out of the window the second we get home, including your mobile phones!' she yelled so loud even I jumped.

'It's his brother,' the twins shouted in unison.

'Fucking Kai,' I snapped and stood up. 'I know who it is. I'll take it from here. Don't think I won't be back to discuss this with you, Mr Hardiman. And thank you for telling the truth boys.'

I stormed out of the office, leaving Mr Hardiman gaping like a fish. He was a stupid, weak man. I could never understand how he got a promotion to head teacher. I'd barely reached the end of the first corridor before I called Alex. His voicemail kicked in by the time I reached the gates of the school playground.

'Harry's gone. Call me urgently, please.' My own calm voice surprised me. I hadn't thought about the Arracht since the twins mentioned the man Harry was speaking to. Maybe I was finally becoming a normal, capable adult. *I will find Harry. We will move away. We will put this mess behind us.*

I had no time to sit around in fear, and the shadow didn't return.

Summer

Three hours had passed since Swanson and I left the cafe. I stood against the kitchen counter, though the white units were too bright for the headache that was starting at the base of my skull. I don't know why I'd mentioned finding my brother to Aaron. If he hadn't texted me, I could have given up searching for him. I wouldn't know if he was OK, but he wouldn't be able to hurt us. God knows Joshua and I deserved a quiet life after everything that happened with Marinda.

I'd finished at Anfield Hospital for the day, but Joshua was sleeping at his dad's house so I was alone. It was only 4 p.m., and I was looking at an evening of catching up on chores. I sighed, pulled out the kitchen chair, and placed my laptop and phone on the table. My tired eyes glazed over as I stared at the flowery welcome message, waiting for the ancient computer to boot up. The vibration of my mobile phone was a welcome distraction. My eyes flicked over to the phone as Aaron's name appeared on the screen. My interest piqued. I grabbed the phone and opened his message. It said nothing other than an address.

The laptop finally kicked into gear, so I opened Google as quickly as the old technology would allow and typed in the address. It was fifteen minutes away, on the other side of town. I replied to Aaron with one word: 'Eddie?'

His reply arrived a few seconds later: 'Yes.'

I jumped up and grabbed my purse, phone and keys, texting Swanson as I left to tell him I'd found Eddie and the address. As I ran down the grand staircase to the main exit, my phone rang.

Swanson didn't even say 'hello'. 'Are you going there now?'

The abruptness of his voice threw me. I froze halfway down the stairs. 'Yes.'

'I'm near your flat. Stay there. I'll pick you up.' He hung up.

What the hell was that about? As strange as it was, I walked outside and stood at the edge of the car park to wait. I supposed I'd prefer to go with a police officer, anyway. I raised my hood against the light drip of rain. Frizzy hair was the last thing I needed if I was going to meet Swanson.

A couple of minutes later, his black Audi approached along the main road, and he pulled up on the opposite side. The same feelings arose every time I saw Swanson: excitement and nerves. I jogged over to get out of the rain.

'Hello again,' I said, a little breathless from the jog. Jesus, I needed to run more often.

'Hey,' he flashed a quick smile, but did not appear to be in a good mood as he pulled away. He took a left at the end of my road into the main traffic.

'You OK?' I asked. It felt weird to ask him that. He always seemed so calm and collected.

'There's a big case at work...' he began, but paused as a driver swerved into our lane. He didn't speak for a few moments as he focused on missing the young driver.

'The rapist case?' I prompted.

'Yep. That's the one.'

'What are you doing here with me, then?'

He turned his head and gave me a sharp look. 'Well, there are a lot of excellent officers on the case. An entire team, in fact. And there's only one of you to help your brother. I can give you one hour tops, then I'm gone.'

I nodded, and we said little for the rest of the drive. Instead, I googled the hospital. Adrenna had transferred Eddie to a low security mental health hospital near Dale Abbey. The new hospital was for people getting ready to move back into the community, like a halfway house for patients rather than criminals. Well, some of them had a violent past like Eddie, but the doctors didn't consider them dangerous anymore.

I wasn't paying any attention to the road as I read my phone, so it surprised me when Swanson stopped the car. I glanced up. The street looked like any other upper-middle-class street. Rows of substantial, mismatched houses. Some were modern, and some were extensive period homes. Eddie's new hospital hid within a classical property that was larger than most homes on the street, thanks to a two-storey extension. There were no high walls or anything else to barricade the patients in. Nobody would know it was a hospital at all from the outside, except for the sign which welcomed you to *Bracken Tree*, with an accompanying NHS logo. Like most of these low security hospitals I've seen, there was a large drive and the house itself sat far back from the road, more so than many other houses.

'Are you ready?' Swanson's rough voice broke me out of my daydream.

I tore my gaze away from the hospital to look at him. 'What should I say?'

'Is Eddie here?' Swanson grinned at me.

'They aren't just going to let me in,' I rolled my eyes.

'No, but they'll let me in,' he flashed his ID card at me.

'Will that work?' I asked.

'Sure, it usually does.'

'OK. Let's go.' A strong breeze met me as I opened the car door, and I pulled my hood back up to protect my hair. As we walked up the long driveway, I kept my head down and tried to ignore my cocktail of emotions. I was nervous to see Eddie after so long, excited to help him, and scared of him being anywhere near me or Joshua all at once. We reached the front door and stood still. Swanson stared at me. I didn't move.

'Well, go on, then,' he said.

'Oh, sorry. I thought you were going to do something.'

He laughed. 'This is more your domain than mine. I hate these places.'

'OK, fine.' I relented and pressed the buzzer near the front door.

A young girl wearing a purple *Bracken Tree* t-shirt answered the door. 'Hi. Can I help you?'

I tried hard not to roll my eyes. She was little more than a child, and would not understand how to care for adult men with mental health issues. An underpaid and overworked kid, as usual. The bloody system was broken.

She smiled up at Swanson and ignored me. I didn't blame her. He had that authoritative presence. If he walked into a room, everyone turned to look. I was the opposite.

'I hope so. I'm Detective Inspector Alex Swanson.' He flashed his badge.

Her eyes widened, though her smile didn't falter.

'I'm looking for Eddie Thomas. Is he in?'

It took her a moment to speak. 'Er, I'm not sure. I'll check.

Do you want to come in?'

I absolutely did not want to enter, but Swanson walked straight inside. I followed with a pounding heart. *Am I about to meet Eddie for the first time in twenty years?*

We stood out of place in the entrance hall as the girl wandered off down the corridor and through a door at the end. In contrast to Adrenna, the hall was lively and modern. Bright white walls complemented light wooden flooring. A notice board took up most of the wall, full of leaflets about different social activities. As we waited, a middle-aged woman descended the stairs in front of us. She took one step at a time, humming as she went. She didn't look up until she was halfway down, stopping abruptly as soon as she spotted us.

'Who are you?' she asked, her voice gruff.

'I'm an advocate,' I smiled up at her before Swanson could answer.

'Oh,' her voice was suddenly much lighter, 'are you here to see me?' She sounded like a little girl now and cocked her head to one side.

I shook my head.

She glared at me before stomping back up the stairs just as the young girl re-entered through the end door. She threw Swanson a nervous glance, as if scared of upsetting him. 'Eddie's not here.'

Relief flooded me.

'That's OK. Miss...?' Swanson said.

'Stacey Bean,' the girl twisted a strand of hair around her finger as she answered.

'Miss Bean.' He smiled. He could look super charming when he wanted to. 'We'll need to look around his room briefly.'

She nodded, glanced behind her and pulled on her hair

145

harder. 'My manager is out with the patients. I just called her but she didn't answer. At the minute it's only me and one other patient who didn't want to go out. She's a talker. Has she seen you?'

'It will only take a minute. It's very urgent, though I can't explain why. You'd be helping us massively,' Swanson said.

The girl sighed and nodded. She walked back down the corridor and motioned for us to follow her. She led us through the property until we reached the rear door leading to the back garden. Across the patio were three self-contained flats.

She led us to the middle one. 'This is Eddie's room. Please be quick. If any patient sees you in there, then we'll be in all sorts of trouble. We need them to trust us, not think random people are searching their rooms while they're not here.'

She unlocked the door but clearly our visit didn't please her. Which gave me a small amount of faith in her, though she was still allowing two strangers into the room. I was pretty sure she could have refused us entry. Swanson hadn't been clear about whether he was allowed to do this or not.

We nodded and entered the room, closing the door behind us to lessen the chance of being spotted by the remaining patient.

I took in the room slowly. It was spotless. Not an item was out of place. There was a single bed, a miniscule kitchen area that was within the same space as the 'lounge', and another door off the back that must have been the bathroom. This was *my* Eddie's room, his private space. I wanted to simultaneously run away from it and explore it. Yet, I didn't move. It wasn't right, being in there without him knowing. I didn't want to see his things yet, not until he was ready to show me, if he ever was.

Swanson strolled around easily. I guessed he was used to

looking through other people's things, both their lives and their belongings. He wandered to the end of the room and stood over a desk. He looked for a few seconds, then walked away. But something made him snap his neck back. He turned to me, mouth partly open.

'What?'

'Shit,' he muttered, reaching for his phone.

'Are you going to tell me what's wrong?'

'Voicemail. I need to listen to this.' He lifted his hand to show he'd be one minute, and raised his phone to his ear. I stood staring at him, and I watched his face whiten.

What the hell was *Alex Swanson* scared of?

Sophie - October 2009

Sophie stood in the middle of the living room. She didn't know where to turn, where to look. Ben sat on the sofa in front of her. His calmness made it worse. His betrayal caught in her chest and manifested into a deep internal pain. It was a heartache that would never go away. She couldn't even cry. Tears wouldn't help, anyway.

'I never thought you would do this to me.' Her voice was barely audible.

'We haven't had sex in ages, Sophie. I *am* sorry, but what did you expect? She threw herself at me and it was over in like one minute. It was stupid.'

'I know we haven't had sex lately. I just thought you felt bad, you know, after what happened. I thought you'd let me know when you wanted it.'

'Felt bad?' he looked confused.

'Yes, because the last few times we had sex, you... were kinda rough,' She couldn't think of the right words to use.

'I thought you liked it rough! Fucks sake, Sophie. If you didn't like it, just say. That's not my fault.'

Sophie said nothing. She didn't mind rough sex. She didn't mind that he lost his temper sometimes. Everyone had flaws. She hated that he hadn't touched her in weeks. Being ignored and not understanding why was far worse than any other punishment. But now she understood why. He'd been with someone else.

'Was it just one time, with you and this woman?'

He answered instantly. 'Yes.' He looked away and rubbed the back of his head. He always did that when he lied.

The room spun. Sophie closed her eyes. She knew what was coming. 'Please, Ben, tell me the truth.'

'OK. It happened twice. The first time, I don't even know what happened, babe. I'd just turned up to do the job in her kitchen. The next minute she was all over me and it had happened before I knew it. And it happened again before I left.'

'And that's it?'

'Well, I had to finish the job the next day, and I said no, babe. I didn't *want* to hurt you. But she got naked and begged me. It was honestly all Kathy.'

Sophie barely listened. A shadow had grown on the wall behind Ben. The Arracht had returned and was reaching its bony hand out to Ben. She stared at it as he prattled on with his excuses, and a strange calmness overcame her. It was like a river. It started at the top of her head and ran down to her toes. The calm quenched the pain in her heart like a painkiller. This emaciated demon of death should terrify her, but he was on her side. She could see that now. The article she'd read was wrong.

The Arracht hovered over Ben, the bony hand near his neck, and she smiled.

'What are you smiling at?' Ben turned to see where she was looking.

'You won't see her again, will you?' Sophie's voice was

149

normal again.

'What? No, of course not,' Ben looked at her and looked behind him again, trying to follow her eyes. 'Er... are you OK?'

'If you do, Benjamin Bates, I will leave you. I'll be out of here faster than you fucked her. Do not fucking test me,' It was the first time she had stood up to Ben in a long time, and it felt good.

He let out a stifled laugh. He stopped when he saw her face. She had felt unsure of herself for so long, but the Arracht was on her side.

She wasn't alone anymore.

Astrid

It had been three hours since Harry went missing. The sky had turned black and the wind howled, shaking the living room window. I stared through the glass, praying Harry was somewhere safe and warm.

It wasn't lost on me that the first 24 hours were crucial in a missing person case, and I should be out looking for him. Yet I'd looked everywhere I could think to look. I'd checked his friends' houses, the football field and the youth club where we practiced Taekwondo. I rang Kai over and over. Harry's phone was now switched off.

It was so different from when Ben went missing all those years ago. I remembered little about his disappearance. I just *knew* he would not come back, and I was unexpectedly calm about it. It seemed strange to admit it now, but it hadn't felt unusual to me.

I lost a part of me that day, and the Arracht became a new companion, always with me. That was the day it grew into a dark force that would stay by my side.

Maybe I was calm then because I had Harry to concentrate on. He was just a tiny baby, and he needed me. I had to be calm and together for his sake. Now, I had no one to focus on. Without Harry, I would be lost forever.

The pain in my heart was too much to bear. I had to find him and make sure he was safe. There was no other alternative.

The only good thing about it being likely that he was with Kai was that I genuinely didn't think Kai would hurt him. God knows what sort of lies Kai was filling Harry's head with, though.

I stood in my living room, just staring. Staring at nothing.

The sound of the door handle made my head snap around.

'Harry?' I rushed to the door and flung it open.

It didn't cross my mind to check the camera.

I saw Harry first and relief flooded me. His tear-streaked face looked up at me and I reached out to comfort him, but he pushed me away and turned away.

It was then that I realised another person was standing next to him. Harry pointed up at him.

'This is my brother, Kai.' Harry's voice cracked as he looked at me accusingly. 'And now I know you've been lying to me my whole life.'

I tried to grab Harry's hand, but he pushed me again. 'Not until you tell me the truth!' he shouted.

'Harry, that is not your brother,' I whispered.

The man let out a stifled, short laugh. His half-hidden face was familiar to me, though I was certain it wasn't Kai.

Harry's face flushed with anger, more than I'd ever seen before. 'Stop lying to me!' he fumed.

'I'm not lying. You have a brother. He looks just like your dad, Harry. He was here yesterday to ask me if he could meet you. Look at me, Harry. *This* man is not your brother.'

The man finally spoke. 'She's lying.'

'I am not!'

'You lied to me about having a brother, Mum! How can I

believe you now? Why would you lie to me in the first place?'

'Lying and omitting information are not the same thing. I will call your brother right now, Harry. It is not this man.' I pulled my phone out of my pocket. Stupid mistake.

The man grabbed my phone from my hand and pushed Harry through the doorway, straight into my stomach. He winded me hard, and we both sprawled on the floor.

He rushed inside and slammed the front door behind him. I jumped up and pulled Harry up off the floor. My hands shook, but I ran down the corridor into the kitchen, dragging a stunned Harry with me by his hoodie.

The man took his time following us.

Harry pulled away from me and turned to face him.

'Harry, come on!' I yelled.

He ignored me and spoke to the man. 'Hey, why'd you push me?'

'To get you inside. You wanted the truth, didn't you? Sorry if I hurt you, mate,' he replied.

I now stood by the back door, but Harry was a couple of feet away, between the man and I.

'We're leaving,' I demanded to Harry, turning to unlock the back door.

'No, Mum.' He turned to face me. 'I need to know the truth.'

'Let's go somewhere to talk, then!' I said.

'No! I want you to tell me here in front of Kai. No more lies.'

'That isn't Kai, Harry! I don't know who the hell he is. Probably the person who's been terrorising me with notes and calls!'

Harry's face dropped. 'That wasn't Kai. I just called once. I only wanted the truth. I wasn't terrorising you.'

'What are you talking about?' I stopped fiddling with the

back door and turned to him.

'The call? And the note. That was me.' Harry looked up at me. 'I'm sorry if I scared you. I felt so guilty after the call. Kai doesn't want to hurt us Mum. I just wanted you to tell me the truth.'

'That was you? Did this man put you up to it? Did Kai put you up to it?' I remembered Harry made me breakfast the morning after the call, and told me he loved me before running into school.

'He asked me to put the note through the door. I got an older kid at school to do it for a fiver.'

I choked back tears, determined not to let the stranger see me cry. 'Jesus, Harry. I've been worried sick about that damn note.'

It all slotted together. I'd known for a while something was wrong with Harry. Then it hit me where I knew the stranger from.

'Yeah, well, you shouldn't have murdered my dad and hid my brother from me.' Harry looked so small suddenly, his bottom lip pouted out just like when he was a toddler. My precious baby still, even at eleven years old.

'I did not murder him. This man has been filling your head full of lies. Which is why I didn't tell you about Kai in the first place. Not that this man is Kai. His name is Charles. He's been sniffing around Barb. Kai knows I didn't murder your dad.'

'OK, it is true.' The man shrugged. 'I'm not Kai. But my name is not really Charles either. Harry has a brother called Kai, though, yes?'

'Yes. I've established that already,' I said shortly, 'are you his friend?'

Harry finally took a step towards me. I reached out and

154

pulled him closer to me, wrapping both arms around him.

'No. I'm Harry's friend.' The man took out a large carving knife from his sleeve. 'Because you murdered their father, Sophie, and it's time to admit it.'

Sophie - June 2010

What began as Sophie's worst nightmare became a dream come true. At least for a bit. The tiny newborn boy curled up in a Moses basket next to their bed.

It took five grand to pay off Kathy in the end, but it was worth it. She had wanted an abortion. It was Sophie's idea to pay her to keep it. An unofficial surrogate was better than no baby. Now, Sophie and Ben's life was complete. It was the perfect plan.

And eight months later, the plan came together. Sophie's editing qualification turned out to be quite lucrative. She'd earned over two thousand pounds from one gig and a few hundred from some others. She had never seen Ben so happy.

Harry was two weeks old, and the deal was done. She was finally a mother. It was difficult to stop looking at his tiny nose and tiny fingers. Most new mothers online were moaning about how tired they were, yet Sophie lay awake at night staring at him, wishing he'd wake up so she could have another cuddle. She was desperate to get to know him. *Would he be funny, or shy, or loud, or cuddly, or a good eater?* He would definitely eat his vegetables and love reading, she'd make sure of that.

Ben was so helpful. He knew what to do since he already had Kai. Though he told her not to pick Harry up when he cried at night so he didn't get too spoiled. She picked him up anyway. Ben was fast asleep, so he wouldn't know.

That night, it was 2 a.m. by the time Harry stirred. His tiny arms and legs kicked out, and his eyes and mouth scrunched up. Sophie grabbed him just as he opened his mouth to wail. She snuck into the spare room where the mini fridge and bottle warmer sat, and settled in the armchair to feed him back to sleep. Ben said she needed to stop night feeds after six weeks, as that was best for Harry. Otherwise he'd be reliant on her at night time. She didn't agree, but Ben was hard to argue with. He'd probably forget what he said anyway. Just in case, she wanted to make the most of such special moments. Maybe she could convince Ben otherwise.

She stroked Harry's tiny hand as he suckled on the bottle. His fingers curled around her little finger and her heart swelled. She'd been worried she'd see Kathy in him, but he was Ben's double, and she would do anything to protect him. No harm would come to Harry under her watch.

Thirty minutes later he was still feeding, and an uneasy feeling crept over her. Ben wouldn't be happy if he woke up and she wasn't next to him.

A creak came from somewhere in the house. Sophie froze. *Was Ben awake?*

She stopped breathing as she listened. Yet the only noise was the quiet suckling of Harry's feeding. Her heart hammered and she willed it to be quiet. She looked down and noticed Harry's eyes were closed and he was suckling in his sleep. Gently, she pressed her little finger into the corner of his mouth to detach him from the bottle teat and stood as quietly as she could. She stood still for a moment, listening for any movements in the bedroom. Nothing.

She snuck across the hall to the bedroom. Ben liked to sleep with the door open, so she didn't have to worry about it making a noise. She placed Harry back in the Moses basket and turned around. Fear slapped her in the face as Ben's eyes stared back at her. His nostrils flared. His eyes flashed with anger.

'Where the fuck were you?' he asked, not even trying to be quiet. He was going to wake Harry.

'Harry woke up,' she stammered, 'he needed feeding. I didn't want him to wake you.'

Ben flung the covers off and stood.

Sophie took a few steps back to ready herself for whatever was about to happen. To her surprise, Ben walked over to her and put his arms around her in a hug. She shivered under his arms, unable to hide her fear. They had been happy for months now, waiting for little Harry. But it had been stressful for Ben.

'Why are you shaking?' he let go of her and stood back to look at her face in the moonlight glow. 'Are you scared of me?'

Sophie didn't know what to say. She knew it made him angry when she showed fear. It was silly when he was just hugging her. She looked up at him. Words strangled in her throat.

'I said, are you scared?' he said again, quieter this time.

Still, she didn't answer.

'I gave you a baby, even tell you how to look after it, and you *ignore* me, then think *I'm* the bad guy?'

'No... no... I'm sorry Ben, really. I'm just new to being a mum. I'm excited. I just wanted to cuddle him. He looks just like you. He's gorgeous.'

'Yeah, well. He wasn't going to look like you, was he?'

Sophie felt an ache in her heart stronger than any pain she'd felt before. It wasn't pain; it was anger. A rage she'd never known before seeped through her. She knew she wasn't perfect, but she'd tried so hard to make Ben happy. If a baby wasn't the answer, then what was?

Before she knew it, Ben grabbed her by the hair. She yelled out in pain, and he slapped her across the face, one hand still full of her hair. Her legs buckled as she tried to stay upright while he yanked her.

'Shut the fuck up,' he growled, 'you'll wake him. Stay silent.'

He bent her over the mattress by her hair and pushed her face into the bed. He spat in his hand before forcing himself inside her. She bit the duvet to keep silent. Harry's perfect little face looked at her from the other side of the bed, between the bars of the cot. His eyes closed. *How could he do this in front of Harry? What was wrong with him?*

Then she looked up. The Arracht had arrived. It had grown bigger than she'd ever seen it, and it's ugly face was enraged.

A calmness ran through her, as it had the day she'd found out about Kathy. She barely felt what was happening. *She* wasn't the problem. Ben was. And she was going to make sure Harry's eyes never opened to his dad hurting his mum. Harry was going to be better than this.

The Arracht circled the ceiling, bits of his rotten flesh dripped down to the bedroom floor. The stench was strong, Sophie couldn't believe Ben couldn't smell it.

Ben was ready to finish and grabbed her hair to drag her to the floor. She obeyed as quickly as she could and opened her mouth like she knew he wanted. Darkness covered the room. The Arracht turned and flew straight towards her. Sophie screamed as it flew inside her. It's dark presence engulfed

159

her. It gave her a new strength born from a manic rage which consumed all other thoughts.

As Ben forced himself into her throat, she bit down hard.

He screamed louder than Sophie had ever heard anyone scream in her life and backhanded her across the face. She released her jaw and turned to grab the nail scissors from the bedside table before launching herself at him.

She threw her arm back and felt the scissors enter his flesh. Then everything went black.

Astrid

'**G**et under the table,' I ordered, though Harry didn't move. I pushed him instead over to the left of the kitchen, away from both of us.

'Stay where you are,' Charles growled.

Beams of autumn sunlight shone through the kitchen window and lingered on the edge of the knife. It was almost pretty. I laughed.

Charles and Harry both stared at me.

'What's so funny, Sophie?' Charles asked.

'Haven't you wondered why I'm not shaking in my boots? Here you are, a big six-foot tall man with a knife in his hand, and yet I'm not scared at all,' I said, as smugly as I could.

He faltered, his arm sagged. His confidence disappeared.

The Arracht hovered above him, flesh dripping to the floor.

'Why do you think I'm not scared, eh? Take a guess.'

'You're not well. The knife is to protect me, not to hurt you. The last time someone tried to get you medical help, you stabbed him to death.'

'Oh, really? Please tell me where you heard such a ridiculous story?' I asked.

'A friend.'

'A friend. Really? Well, they're lying. For your information,

I'm fine. I have never been mentally unwell, but I can be dangerous when it comes to protecting Harry. Now, get the fuck out of my house while you can still walk.'

'If you're so dangerous, why not just kill me now? Because it would prove me right? That you are a murderer.'

'Because I'd rather *not* in front of my child. Unless I have to. And I'd rather not have to move another body.' I shrugged. I felt Harry's wide eyes on me, but I didn't take my stare off Charles.

'So you did kill Ben, then?' His eyes glinted with satisfaction.

'Who said I was talking about Ben?' I laughed again. I was quite enjoying fucking with him.

His eyes squinted in confusion or anger, I wasn't sure which.

I primed every part of my body in case he moved forward. I knew if I could throw him off-guard then I'd stand a better chance of winning in a physical fight. I've won plenty of sparring matches at Taekwondo. I'd already worked out which hand to hold his knife away with and which foot to swing around his head.

'Have you ever actually killed somebody?' I asked, trying to fuck with him further. 'Have you felt their last breath leave their body? Their death rattle will stay with you forever.' I did a raspy breath to show him what I meant. I tried not to think about the fact that I was terrifying poor Harry, who cowered at my side. Instead, I concentrated only on the monster in front of me.

His face was pale. This wasn't playing out how he wished.

I kept going. 'Have you tried to move a dead body? They're heavy, you know. I'm sure you've heard of 'dead weight'. And then there's the CSI stuff. You've probably left hair all over already.'

162

The man looked around him as if he would see any hair that had fallen from his head.

'They can tell how tall the attacker was from the blood splatter, whether you're right or left-handed,' I said.

He gulped. 'Shut up! I don't want to kill anybody. I want to help. You just need to tell the truth.' He was losing it. I had to be careful he didn't attack us out of fear.

'Just leave now and I will move away. Then we can both forget this happened,' I said.

'No. You just admitted you killed him. I know you had issues, but you need help to face up to it. That isn't an excuse to hurt people. You have to pay.' The man's eye twitched.

'Do you deserve to go to prison?' I asked.

'Why?' he looked like he might cry.

'Because you will if you don't put the knife away and get out.' I gestured towards the knife. 'Either that, or you'll die.' I ran to Harry and grabbed my handbag on the counter, reaching inside.

'Stop!' yelled Charles.

But I couldn't stop. My body moved without me telling it to. I had no control.

And my vision was going black once more.

Summer

We need to get back in the car,' Swanson said as he turned and ran out of Eddie's room.

I rushed after him, slamming Eddie's flat door shut behind us without a second look. I was glad to leave, though God knows where the hell we were rushing to.

'Where are we going?' I asked as we reached the main house's corridor.

'I'll explain on the way.' His urgency must have been obvious as we reached the front door, because Stacey opened it as soon as she saw us running. Swanson ran through the open door without saying a word.

'Thanks for your help.' I smiled at her as we ran past.

She said nothing in reply and just stared at us.

We reached the car, and I fell into the front seat, trying to keep up with Swanson. He sped off down the street, still not telling me what the emergency was.

'What's spooked you?' I asked.

'I don't know where to start.' He sighed. 'It's a bit of a long story. A woman I know just left me a voicemail. She rang me the other day too. Someone has been accusing her of things. Leaving her notes and calling her in the middle of the night. Now, her eleven-year-old son is missing.'

'Oh no.' I gasped, and my hand flew to my stomach. The thought of Joshua going missing made me feel instantly sick. 'Do you want to kick me out while you go to her? I can get a bus back.'

'Nope. I think I'm going to need you with me.' He threw me a glance as he sped around a corner.

'What? why?' I wish he'd just spit out the complete story.

'I've just seen pictures of this same woman, and her missing son, in your brother's room.'

It's a good job I was sitting already, as I felt my legs go weak. I opened my mouth to speak but only a strangled noise came out. No. It couldn't be true. I turned to glare at Swanson.

'He's not dangerous anymore. That's why they transferred him there. He wouldn't hurt her son,' I snapped. I knew it was weak. I'd worked in low security places as a support worker before I became an advocate. I knew some patients there were absolutely still dangerous. Even so, I didn't care. My brother was not dangerous to random children.

'Summer, you don't know your brother. I know what Marinda said about him not actually being ill, but perhaps he is now. He's been locked away and told he was crazy for twenty years. That's enough to drive anyone nuts.'

I kept my mouth shut at his use of the word 'nuts'. He was right about Eddie though. I didn't know him at all, other than some vague childhood memories. The most vivid of these was him trying to kill Mum.

'Why would he take a child?' I asked. 'It makes no sense.'

Swanson said nothing in reply.

It took ten minutes to reach the destination, a beautiful detached house on Rose Way. Swanson abandoned the car across the street and ran up the drive. He banged on the front door. I followed him and stood awkwardly at the end of the drive.

Nobody answered the door. Swanson knocked again.

'She's probably not in. I'd be out looking for Joshua if it was me. Let's go.' I looked over at Swanson. I hadn't seen him like this before. He seemed to be in a world of his own, agitated yet zoned out.

Just then, a bang ripped through the house, so loud that the front door shook.

'Shit! Get down, Summer!' Swanson lifted his mobile to his ear but I couldn't hear what he said.

Someone screamed inside the house.

An image of Joshua appeared in my mind and I ducked behind the driveway fence in an attempt to move to safety. I had to stop getting into dangerous situations.

Swanson put the phone back in his pocket. 'I'm going in. Go to the car.' He ran into the house without waiting for my response.

But the pictures Eddie had flew through my mind. If Eddie was in there hurting somebody then I needed to help.

Swanson

S wanson jumped back behind the front door. He poked his head around the frame to see who had the gun.

A man stood in the kitchen doorway at the end of the corridor, blood splattered across his shirt. Behind the man stood Sophie.

The man spotted Swanson and instantly he raised his arms in the air. Swanson heard a clatter as something hard fell from the man's hand.

'Help!' Sophie screamed. Tears streaked her face. Her eyes were wild.

Swanson moved into the house and stayed low behind the stairs. 'Where is the gun?' he yelled out.

'It's here. I won't shoot. Just please help.' Sophie was inconsolable and barely got the words out. She was even worse than the night Ben had gone missing.

Swanson stuck his head around the base of the stairs. The man blocked the kitchen doorway with two empty hands held in the air.

'Move,' Swanson said to the man, pointing to the far end of the kitchen. The man did as he was told.

'Eddie?' a voice asked in a whisper.

Swanson startled; he hadn't noticed Summer sneak in

behind him.

The man's neck snapped round to look at her. His pale face whitened further. His mouth half opened, and he took a few steps forward.

'Move!' Swanson was more threatening this time, and the man instantly stepped to the side of the kitchen.

Sophie dropped to her knees, sobbing over a silent small figure on the floor. Harry. Thick blood seeped from his side.

'I shot him, I shot him,' Sophie continued to wail.

Swanson ran over and pushed her away from Harry. He knelt over the boy. There was so much blood it was hard to tell where the wound was.

'I already called for an ambulance. Where was he shot?' Swanson said.

Sophie shook her head through her sobs. The pool of blood was mainly to Harry's left side, so Swanson set to work finding the wound and applying pressure.

'Eddie?' Summer repeated as she entered the kitchen.

'Summer,' Swanson snapped, 'come here and help me hold pressure on the wound. It's his arm.' He pointed at Eddie. 'You stay there.'

Summer startled as though she'd only just noticed the injured boy. She immediately dropped to the floor to help. Harry wasn't fully conscious. His eyes flickered open and closed. His small body shook. Sophie ran back over and sat above his head to stroke his hair.

'I'm sorry, baby. It's OK. It's OK. You're gonna be OK.'

Swanson could hear distant sirens, and it wasn't long before paramedics ran inside the house. Summer and Swanson moved out of the way and let the specialists work on Harry. Swanson turned to find Eddie, but he was nowhere to be seen.

Summer

I ran outside to look for Eddie as soon as the ambulance crew arrived to care for the boy. It had only taken a few minutes for the ambulance to arrive, yet Eddie was gone. Swanson followed me out. My whole body shook as I turned to him, and I put a hand near my mouth as I felt the nausea rise.

'There,' Swanson pointed to a drain.

I ran over and threw up. I lifted my hands to wipe my mouth. The child's blood was all over them. Blood covered my trousers, too. The pavement spun. I grabbed the kerb for support.

I didn't hear him coming, but Swanson's powerful hands lifted me up and sat me down properly. 'Put your head between your knees. You're in shock,' he ordered.

I did as I was told without question. I heard commotion and sirens but took no notice of what was happening. Seeing Eddie had shocked me, but that poor boy covered in blood would stay with me forever. His mother's screams would never leave me.

'He's in the best place now, Summer.' Swanson was looking down at me. 'Come on, let's get you home.'

Swanson gave me a lift home, much to Hart's disdain.

She'd turned up just as the ambulance arrived and wanted to question me straight away. Swanson and I didn't speak much on the drive. He helped me up to my flat and promised to call as soon as he knew more about what had happened.

I showered and sat in my empty flat to wait. The telly was on in the background. The noise was comforting, though I didn't watch it. Joshua was still at his dad's house for the night, and would be meeting his baby sister. I thought I'd feel jealousy, or at least a little emotional. Yet the shock of the day's events clung on. It felt like a weird dream. Had I really just seen the aftermath of a mother who shot her own child?

After two hours of on and off dozing on the sofa, my doorbell finally rang.

'Hey, it's me.' Swanson's voice crackled through the intercom and I buzzed him through the main entrance. I opened my flat door to wait for him.

'Did you find him?' I asked as he stepped into the corridor. He shook his head. I moved aside to let him in. We made our way to the kitchen. 'Is Harry going to be OK?'

'We'll see.' Swanson leant against the kitchen counter. He never sat or accepted a drink, so I didn't bother to offer.

'And it really was Astrid who shot him?' I asked.

He nodded and rubbed his beard. 'Accidentally.'

'I guess she'll be in trouble whether or not it was an accident? I've had no one call me for a statement yet.'

Swanson looked away. 'I need to talk to you about that.'

'What about it? Will you take the statement?' I asked.

Swanson shook his head. 'There's something I need to tell you.'

Swanson June 2010

Swanson woke covered in sweat, and his ears ringing. He jumped out of bed and flicked on the lamp. Either someone's screams nearby had woke him, or he was dreaming.

He stood still, listening out for any signs of trouble. A thud came from next door, but they were never quiet. Ben was always yelling, and now there was a baby added into the mix.

Swanson went round once after Ben invited him to a BBQ. His wife was nice, if a little quiet, but Ben was a cocky bellend. Swanson had only returned on one occasion since: a night when the shouting got so bad that he'd felt compelled to check on Sophie. She was out, or at least that's what Ben had said.

He didn't want to get too involved. He'd been there with his own parents. It never ended well.

He strained his ears. Could he hear grunting noises? *Christ, was he listening to Ben and Sophie having sex?* He rubbed his eyes and flicked off the light, ready to sleep again. Before he could lie back down, a deep scream made him snap the light back on.

Rather than the usual high-pitched screams, this time it was a man's yell. Adrenaline pumped through him as he threw on the jeans and jumper from the floor of his bedroom and ran outside to the front garden. Once outside he stood still and still peered over his fence at their house.

Was he overreacting? Were they just fighting again?

The hairs on his arms raised despite the unusually humid summer night. There were no more screams, but something wasn't right.

He walked up the path. At least if he knocked, he would know they were OK. As he raised his hand to bang on the front door, it flew open and Sophie appeared with the baby in her arms.

'Hey, Sophie. You OK? I heard a shout.' He looked behind her for Ben. She was shaking with tears, sobbing too hard to answer him. Fresh blood stained her nightdress.

'Come on. Come with me.' He put his hand on her shoulder and led her down the path into his house. There was still no sign of Ben. Swanson considered what he should do as an off-duty police officer. Call for backup? That seemed silly. It was just a crying neighbour. What would he say?

Once inside, he realised she was covered in blood. It was all over her top and even dripping down from between her legs. The situation was much more serious than their usual scraps.

'Sophie, what happened?' he spoke quietly and put his hands on her shoulders. She was shaking. 'Let's put the baby down.'

He made a space between cushions on the sofa for the baby and took him from her arms. She didn't fight him. He made her a glass of water as she took deep breaths and tried to calm down enough to tell him what happened.

'Here, sip this. Tell me what happened.'

'He just wouldn't stop. He wouldn't stop,' she said through gasping sobs.

'He hurt you physically? What did he do?' Swanson kept

his voice gentle. He needed to coax the information out of her. Maybe he could get her to open up, and they could get a conviction for Ben. It was almost impossible if the victim didn't give a statement.

'He wouldn't stop. I had to. I had to do it to protect Harry. Don't take Harry from me.' She looked up and her pleading eyes burrowed deep into his.

Swanson gulped. 'Why would I take Harry from you, Sophie? Is Ben OK?'

She slowly shook her head. 'I had to stop him. I had to.'

'Wait here.' Swanson grabbed his house keys and locked the front door behind him as he rushed over to check on Ben.

He prayed Ben wasn't dead. Shit. He was a police officer, for fuck's sake. How could he let this happen to his own neighbour?

His feet crunched over the gravel path to their front door. His radio was at the station, so he had his phone in hand ready to call for backup if needed. He knocked on the front door quietly, trying not to wake any other neighbours.

No answer.

He pushed the handle down and the door popped open easily.

'Hello?' Swanson called out, adrenaline pumping through him. Silence greeted him.

A trail of blood led from the hallway and up the stairs. He snuck up the stairs one at a time, listening for any noise as he went. Once he reached the top of the stairs, he called out again.

It was still silent other than his own blood pounding in his ears. He followed the trail of blood to the main bedroom. Christ, what had she done to cause this much blood?

As he entered the room, the spatter continued along the

floor at the bottom of the bed. He rushed to the other side, full of dread at what he might have allowed to happen.

But the dread turned to a rising panic as he saw what Sophie had done, and he fell to his knees on the bedroom floor. Benjamin Bates lay there, unmoving and freezing cold.

Summer

Swanson looked down at the floor as he spoke. It made no sense to me that someone like Swanson would bend any rules. Ever. He was always so stoic and straight-laced.

'So you helped her get away?' I asked.

Swanson nodded. 'It was stupid and I'll always regret it. I was young, and new to the job. The fear of another officer finding out what happened... it lives with me every day. I even cleaned up the blood in her house and let her sleep on my sofa for a couple of nights until his family somehow heard he had gone missing. Sophie told me he didn't speak to his family so I didn't think they'd be too much of a problem, to be honest. I thought he could just disappear. I called my aunt then. I knew she had a house that needed a tenant and I dropped off Sophie and Harry and paid their deposit.'

'Do you think she forgot what she did?' I asked.

'Well, it seems that way. My aunt had been in a similar situation with her first ex-husband, so I told her what happened. My aunt monitored Sophie for me, and they became friends. Yet Sophie tells everyone Ben just randomly disappeared and that he was amazing to her.' He shrugged. 'She seems to have no memory of either of them hurting each other at all. The family tried to find her. They were unsuccessful until recently.'

'Didn't the police look for her?' I asked.

He shifted uncomfortably. 'The police don't know. They were never told about any of it.'

'Never told?' I looked away, trying to process the web of what he was telling me.

'He wasn't officially reported missing by his family or by Sophie. She thought she'd reported it to the police via me, but obviously she didn't. I've just allowed her to think that because she seems fine otherwise. I didn't see the point in correcting her. So what if she can't remember what happened? As long as she and Harry are OK. I visited her all the time. We grew apart after... well, after...'

'You broke up?' I answered for him.

His face reddened but he nodded.

'Where the hell does my brother fit in?' I was more bothered about Eddie than any of this strange story, and didn't blame Sophie for forgetting. I already wanted to forget.

'Other than the photos, I have no idea.' He gave me a serious look. 'The photos were taken from far away, as if he'd been watching them.'

'Why would he be watching them?' I spoke more to myself than to Swanson.

He shrugged. We fell into silence for a moment. His mobile phone startled us both when it rang.

'Sorry,' he said, leaving the kitchen to answer his phone.

I sat alone, trying to figure out why on earth my brother would follow this random woman. Well, she was random to me. He obviously knew her somehow. Had they been friends? How could that be the case if he was released from the secure hospital only recently? It was difficult to make friends while locked away, though he must have had unescorted leave before being moved to a low security place.

Swanson returned a couple of minutes later, interrupting my thoughts. 'That was the same aunt I mentioned a minute ago. She needs to see me, something to do with Sophie. I'll call you later.'

I walked him out to the hallway.

He turned to me as he was halfway out the front door. 'Be careful, Summer. We don't know how dangerous your brother might be.'

I nodded, thankful that Joshua wasn't around tonight. I just hoped my brother didn't know where I lived.

Unless he had been following me too?

Swanson

The rain hammered down on the roof of Swanson's car as he drove to Barb's Manor. She hated him calling it that, but there were worse names he could think of for it. It was far too ostentatious. His phone rang and Hart's name flashed up.

'Yes?' Swanson answered.

'Where the fuck are you?' Hart's voice had that hushed urgency she always had when she was angry. Most people raised their voice when mad, but Hart was so loud usually that she seemed to do the opposite.

'I'll be back real soon. Something urgent came up.'

'Er... urgent like the mum shooting her own child that needs to be interviewed? Or urgent like the rapist we need to find?'

'It's to do with the mother, or the guy that was at the scene with her, anyway. I feel like this is all connected. Just trust me, I'll be back soon.'

Hart tutted loudly. Swanson tried not to laugh as he imagined her face turning red.

'Listen, arsewipe. I'm not going down with you. If anyone asks, then I don't know where you are and we never spoke.'

'Of course. Are forensics on the property?'

'The mum's house? Yes. They're nearly done. The bullet

178

was lodged in the kitchen wall. Some blood splatter was in the same area. They've found some prints and hair samples to send off. Forest is at the hospital with the mum. There are a couple of guys out taking statements from neighbours, too.'

'OK, I'll be in soon. Don't interview the mum without me.'

'Call me if you need backup.'

'I'm only going to see a friend. See you soon,' Swanson hung up the phone.

The rain eased off, so he put his foot down to reach the Manor quicker. If he wasn't around to interview Sophie, then someone else might step in, and that was the last thing he needed.

He pulled up to Barb's a few minutes later and ignored the sweeping driveway, opting instead to park on the roadside for a quick getaway if Hart called again. He grabbed his phone and keys and hauled himself out of the Audi, cursing himself for not sticking with the weights. Dodging the larger puddles, he stalked up the driveway and rang her doorbell twice in quick succession. The door flew open seconds later.

'Alex, darling, thank you for coming so quickly. Come in now out of that awful rain.' She waved him inside with a flourish.

'Hi, Barb.' Swanson entered the hallway and she put her hand on his arm to lead him to their usual spot at the kitchen table. Her hands were the only thing which gave away her age. She never admitted exactly how old she was, but she was much older than his fifty-year-old mother.

'Thank you for coming so quickly,' Barb said as they sat on the cushioned marble-effect chairs. Barb had already laid out a water jug and a glass for him.

'Well, it sounded urgent.' ice clattered as Swanson filled a glass from the water jug.

'It's more strange than urgent, I think. I have a friend, Charles, who I met a few weeks ago in Waitrose. We have a lot in common. He dresses and speaks well, you know.'

Swanson sipped his water to hide his grin, though Barb was looking away from him and through the kitchen window.

She continued with her story. 'So we went out for dinner a few days later, and to the library a few days after that. Eventually I thought it would be OK to invite him back here. I had a book he wanted to borrow and he was so nice to me. Astrid called that same day, and she didn't sound too good, so I told her to come over.'

Swanson sat up in his chair and grabbed his notepad and a pen from his pocket.

'What are you doing, dear?' Barb asked.

'Just making notes. I have something to tell you in a minute, but go on.'

'Oh... OK. Well, I introduced them, and then Astrid and I went into the garden. When she left I found him hiding in here, watching her leave through the window. It was unnerving, if I'm honest. He didn't take the book he'd asked to borrow. Then he didn't call again until earlier today. He asked what Astrid had said and if she would be home today. Maybe I'm just being silly, but there are some strange people about, and the whole thing gave me the willies. I didn't want to call Astrid and worry her. So I thought maybe you could take care of it, darling.'

'Take care of it?' Swanson asked.

'Yes, you know. Look into it or something. He also asked if I knew someone called Summer.' She raised her eyebrows and put her palms to the ceiling.

'Summer?' Swanson's chair scraped across the floor as he stood.

'Oh, be careful with the floor there, dear.' Barb seemed unphased by his sudden movement.

'Listen, something happened earlier today with So... Astrid. I can't really go into detail. It involved a man in her home with Harry.'

The colour drained from Barb's face. 'Are they OK?'

'Well, Harry is in hospital, but we think he's going to be fine. Astrid is with him. We need to speak to her to establish what happened. It appears an intruder might have gotten into their home, and in her fight to make sure Harry was OK, she somehow hurt Harry herself. But we need to know who the intruder was.'

'Oh, God. Charles?' Barb put her face in her hands.

'Well, it sounds possible,' Swanson answered.

'Oh my God, I led him right to her,' she said through her fingers, her voice cracked.

'Do you know where he lives?'

'No... I haven't visited his house yet. I do have his number.' She raised her head and walked to the counter to find her mobile phone.

Barb fussed with the login screen on her phone. Christ it would take her ages to find the phone number. Swanson stepped over to her and held out his hand. She passed him the phone and he found the number and jotted it down.

'OK. I need to go, Barb. Thanks for calling. This could really help us. Don't speak to Charles again. If he comes over or contacts you, call me.'

Barb led him back through the hallway, much more subdued than she had been when she let him in. At the front door, she

181

leaned up to him and kissed his cheek. 'Tell Astrid I'm sorry, please?' she said as she pulled away.

'She's OK, Barb. You don't need to be sorry. You've probably really helped us.'

She nodded, yet her face showed his words made her feel no better. Guilt tugged at him as he walked away, but he needed to make sure Summer was safe, and he needed to interview Astrid. His phone rang as soon as he pulled off Barb's street.

'Yes, Hart?'

'You on your way yet, or what? Murray said she'll put Walker on the interview if you're not here within five seconds.'

'For fuck's sake. Yes, I'm coming. Tell her to keep her wig on.'

'Shall I actually?'

'What?'

'Tell her you said to keep her wig on?'

Swanson laughed. 'You wouldn't dare.'

'Meh. You're probably right. It depends how much you piss me off in the next few minutes. The mum is at the hospital, anyway. How quickly can you get there?'

'I'm literally minutes away. I'll probably beat you.'

'Is that a bet?'

'Go on, then. Loser buys coffee.'

'You don't drink coffee.'

Swanson hung up and put his foot down. He tried to call Sophie, but the phone rang out. What the hell would he say to her? He needed to beat Hart to the hospital. He rang her again, but still no answer.

He reached the hospital within a few minutes and abandoned his car on a piece of grass close to the entrance. He'd deal with any parking fine later.

He walked through the smokers outside the entrance and checked out the reception area. It was far too busy to wait in line. An older receptionist stood reading some paperwork at the edge of the desk, not talking to anyone. He walked right up to her. She looked up, clearly annoyed at his intrusion.

He flashed his ID and asked where he could find Harry's ward. Her attitude changed and she was immediately helpful in telling him where to go.

Swanson followed her directions, walking through the maze of corridors and entering the lift twice to reach the correct floor. People milled about everywhere. Kids were running around tired parents and beds which were nearly as wide as the corridor were being wheeled about by porters. It was busy and noisy and everything else Swanson hated. The bustle brought him back to being a child, which was a time he'd much rather forget ever happened.

An ex had once accused him of being born as a grumpy old man. Hart had loved that.

Eventually, he found the correct ward with Forest sitting outside, just like Hart said.

'Forest.' Swanson nodded to him. 'Have you been here the whole time?'

'Swanson.' He nodded back. 'Yeah. Well, I'm trying not to get in the way.'

'OK. Have you got an update?'

Forest gave him a blank look. 'Well, I haven't been inside yet. I'm just making sure the mum doesn't go anywhere and the male suspect doesn't come back.'

'So, your update is that nothing has happened yet?'

Forest nodded again, his face very serious. It was almost comical to see him sitting outside staring at the door. He was older than he looked, but he was fairly inexperienced and not the sharpest tool in the box.

Swanson rang the ward bell to get the nurse's attention. She smiled and pressed the buzzer to unlock the ward door for him, waving him inside.

At the reception desk, he flashed his ID to the nurse. 'I'm here to get an update on the condition of Harry Moor, and speak to his mother.'

'Oh, OK. Harry's near the end of the ward. He's doing fine, just a nasty cut, really, but he's resting. I think the shock was worse than the wound. His mum is with him.'

Swanson nodded, ignoring the other nurses who edged closer to listen to their conversation. He smiled and thanked the nurse and headed in the direction she pointed.

He saw the back of Sophie's red hair before anything else, shining like a beacon.

She didn't move when he reached her and continued to stare at Harry instead. The boy lay fast asleep on his back in the bed, his breath steady and rhythmic.

'Astrid?' Swanson said, as quietly as he could. He placed his hand on her shoulder.

She whipped around.

'Oh, it's you. Why did you call me Astrid?' She turned back to face Harry.

'Well, I need to interview you with a colleague. It's best if we act like strangers, OK? But don't panic, it will be fine. Harry's fine, you're fine, everybody is fine.'

He fell silent. She didn't respond.

'Astrid? Did you hear me?'

'Yes, yes. We don't know each other.' She waved him away and turned back to watch Harry.

'I'll be back soon with another officer and we'll go somewhere to talk, OK?'

She nodded, but still refused to turn to him. Maybe she knew he couldn't help. After all, how could he if she admitted to shooting Harry? Where the hell did the gun even come from?

Swanson left the ward and called Hart. 'I'm outside the ward with Forest. Where are you?'

'Fucking lost in this bastard maze.'

'Well, I guess you're buying coffee.'

'Again, you don't drink coffee.'

'That's not the point. I won it fair and square, so I want coffee. I'll give it to Forest. Do you need directions?'

'Don't give me that pretentious shit that you do, just be nice and give directions like a normal person.'

Swanson laughed loudly, and Forest looked over at him in his nervous way. He gave Hart directions as nicely as he could manage and hung up to wait for her.

'Is everything OK in there?' Forest asked.

'Yes, they're both in there. The boy is going to be fine. It all seems like one big accident.'

'Oh, that's good then.' Forest stood and wandered to the window to look outside. He looked like a skinny child with bum fluff.

They didn't speak. Swanson couldn't be arsed with small talk. He went over every plausible scenario in his head. Could Sophie keep her mouth shut about them? He doubted it. She wasn't exactly on her game right now.

Hart bustled through the corridor doors a few minutes later. She held her head high, as if daring him to say something about needing directions. He wondered whether she could take a joke, but decided against it when he saw her red face. She was

185

pissed.

'Alright?' he asked.

'No, I'm not. I'm sick of chasing you everywhere this week,' she snapped, 'and I've just been sent that list of names from the car place. Guess who's on it as a visiting worker? An electrician?'

'Peter Johnson?' Swanson guessed.

'Yep. So we need to pay him another visit first thing. In there, is she?' she pointed to the ward door.

'Yeah. Listen. I have to tell you something.' He pulled her to one side away from Forest, who wasn't paying any attention, anyway. 'I know the mum. We dated a few years ago.'

'Oh for fuck's sake, Swanson, and you wait until now to tell me.' Hart closed her eyes and put her hand up in front of his face. 'Nope. I didn't just hear that.'

'This is serious, Hart.'

'Forest.' Hart ignored him and walked away. 'You're coming with me, come on.'

She gave Swanson an annoyed look and pressed the bell to the ward. Forest joined her, looking so terrified that it would have been funny in any other circumstance. Poor Forest.

Swanson considered putting his foot down and insisting on going in, but actually if he wasn't there then Sophie was surely less likely to mention their past.

The nurse buzzed Hart and Forest into the ward. Swanson took Forest's seat and crossed his arms. He stared at the ward door, willing it to open again.

They should bring Sophie out of the ward to chat to her somewhere away from her son's sickbed, but as he waited, he realised they weren't going to. Many thoughts ran through his head. Has she refused to speak to them? Has something happened to Harry?

After thirty minutes, they came back outside and he jumped out of his chair to greet them. Forest looked much happier now, clearly relieved it was over.

'So?' Swanson asked Hart.

'Come on, I'll tell you on the way back down. Forest will stay for a bit longer.'

They walked down the corridor and headed towards the exit.

'So, she said Harry disappeared about 1 p.m., which we knew about as the school reported it. He turned up with a man at around 5 p.m. who looked familiar, though she wasn't sure where he was from. The man had a gun and forced his way inside. He wanted money, which she clearly has, but she had no cash on her. She led him to the kitchen to pretend to get some, grabbed the gun and it went off. Which is about when you arrived.'

'Right, well.' Swanson paused. 'I was trying to help a friend find someone.'

'You were trying to help Summer find her brother.'

'How did you know that?'

'I'm good at my job.'

'Meh. You're alright.' Swanson grinned, but stopped when he saw the sharp look on her face. 'OK. So, I think the man at the house was Summer's brother. He had pictures of the mum and the boy in his room at the hospital. So, I went over to check on her. That's what Summer and I were doing there.'

'OK. It's all making a bit more sense now you're finally explaining yourself. So how does he know Astrid?'

'No idea. That's the missing piece right now.'

'OK. Let's go back to the office. We need to sort through

it all. What a fucking mess. I think forensics are finished sweeping the house though, so we should have the tests back pretty quickly.'

'I'll meet you there, I'm going to talk to Summer. If anyone can help us find Eddie, it's her.'

'Fine,' Hart said, though her tone suggested it was anything but.

They left in their respective cars, agreeing to meet at the office. Swanson didn't believe Summer would have any idea where Eddie was, but if he was as dangerous as Sophie suggested then he needed to make sure Summer was safe.

The last thing they needed was anyone else getting hurt.

Astrid

I've always hated hospitals, and avoided the doctor like the plague. I'd been lucky to have no emergencies until now, and Harry was lucky to be alive. It was just a flesh wound, yet it could have been so much worse. And it was all my fault. Other outcomes flashed through my mind. The sick feeling in the pit of my stomach would never go away. We would definitely move now. If Harry even wanted to stay with me.

Kai sat across from me as Harry slept, putting my nerves even more on edge. He'd turned up at the house just as we were leaving in the ambulance, but hadn't visited the hospital until much later. He looked so much like Ben. I knew now why I didn't like being reminded of Ben, why I'd gotten scared when I saw Kai. The memory of Ben's disappearance was too hard to relive.

'So you don't know who that man could have been?' I asked him for the millionth time.

He shook his head.

'I told you, I got a note with your address. I didn't see any man. And I wouldn't see Harry without your say-so. I know I can get angry and say things. But I want him to like me.'

I know I can get angry and say things. The blurred edges of a memory flashed through my mind. I pushed it away before it could form an actual picture.

'When he's better,' I answered.

Kai nodded. 'You'll let me know?'

'Yes. I'll call. He'll want to meet you. Now he knows you exist, and I need him to realise that man wasn't you. You can trust me.'

Kai left soon after. I sat with Harry, watching his rhythmic breathing until his eyes slowly opened. He looked around the room, still groggy from the painkillers.

'Hi baby,' I smiled at him, praying he wouldn't push me away. I blinked away the tears which threatened to fall.

'Hi, Mum.' He reached out for me and I took his hand. 'What happened?'

'Don't panic. Kai had a gun. The bullet hit your arm but it's just a graze. Nothing serious. You're going to be fine,' I said.

He groaned and closed his eyes. 'I don't feel fine.'

'I think you bumped your head on the way down.' I looked at his pale face and stroked his cheek.

'Yeah, I remember the nurse said. Where's Kai now?' he leant into my hand and closed his eyes again.

'He's gone. The police have him.'

He opened his eyes wide and looked at me. 'I'm so sorry, Mum.' His voice cracked and tears brimmed in his eyes.

I couldn't hold mine back any longer. 'Oh, baby. You have nothing to be sorry for. Can you ever forgive me for not telling you about Kai, Harry? I thought he was dangerous.' I sniffed.

He nodded. We hugged gently, though I wanted to squeeze him tight and never let go.

'What really happened to Dad?' his voice was so quiet.

'He really disappeared, babe. The police officer will tell you

190

when he comes.' I kissed his head.

'What if Kai comes back?' he asked, fear in his eyes.

'I don't know, but don't worry. We're going to move for that big job, remember? We'll go to the beach as soon as you're feeling better. And we'll pick a new house, and a puppy. You don't even have to go to school.' I smiled at him. I'd always wanted to home school. 'And you can visit the twins whenever you want. It's all going to be fine.'

It didn't take long for Harry to fall back asleep. I wasn't sure if it was all the stress or the painkillers. If we were going to move, I needed to go home and pack. I flicked open my phone and booked a nice-enough hotel for two weeks in Cornwall. I wasn't staying in Derby a minute longer than I had to.

Harry's cheek was warm and soft as I kissed him goodbye. On my way out, I told the nurse I was leaving to collect some clothes. A police officer stood outside the ward, looking through the window. I buzzed open the ward doors and easily snuck past him.

I raced home as fast as I dared without risking a speeding fine. The last thing I needed was to draw unwanted attention. The driveway was empty when I reached the house, and someone had used the spare key to lock the front door. Luckily I'd instinctively grabbed mine on the way out of the house earlier in the evening.

It was 10 p.m. already, so I raced straight up the stairs to grab the suitcases, completely focussed on getting packed and getting out.

It wasn't until I walked into the living room to put down my first suitcase that I spotted him, sprawled out on the sofa as if already at home.

My husband, and the love of my life, was in my house.

191

Summer

I wound down the window to let the cold breeze wash over me as I drove. Sitting in the flat alone had made me overthink, so I was on my way to the supermarket. I needed to do the shopping before Joshua returned from his dad's house, anyway.

It didn't take long to reach the supermarket. The bright lights were welcoming against the dark evening sky as I pulled up close to the entrance.

I hated dark car parks.

As I entered through the open doors of the shop, my mobile phone vibrated in my jeans pocket. I fished it out and Swanson's name flashed up.

'Hey,' I froze in the middle of the supermarket, attracting filthy looks from shoppers as they tried to get by. I moved to the side of the entrance, trying to look apologetic.

Swanson's voice was more rushed than usual. 'Hey, Summer. Listen, I'm at my aunt's house. She made a friend recently. A man who became strangely interested in Astrid.'

'Whose Astrid?' I asked.

'Sophie — sorry, I didn't mention that she changed her name to Astrid.' He spat out the words as if that was an unimportant detail.

'Oh, OK. Wait… why are you telling me about this man?' my heart raced.

'Well, she has no photos of him, but I think my aunt's new friend might be Eddie. She has his phone number, but I haven't called it yet,' silence hung in the air as the question sat unasked. If he was going to call Eddie, I wanted to be there.

'Do you have time to meet?' I asked.

'Sure. Be at yours in less than half an hour.' He hung up without saying goodbye.

I abandoned my trolley and raced home in less than ten minutes.

I rushed to the bathroom, where a tired and pale face stared back at me in the mirror. I brushed my hair, slicked on some pink lip gloss, and applied concealer to hide the bags under my eyes.

True to his word, Swanson arrived ten minutes later.

I let him upstairs, and he stood awkwardly in the doorway with a half-smile on his face. I waved him inside with a nervous grin.

As we entered the kitchen, he handed me a piece of paper with a phone number and the name 'Charles' in tight, square handwriting.

'Charles?' I looked at him with one eyebrow raised.

'My aunt said that's the man's name.' Swanson shrugged.

'Charles was our father's name,' I said.

Swanson said nothing. I sat at the kitchen table and for once he sat too.

'Do you want to call him?' I asked.

'If you feel comfortable. I think he'd respond better to you.'

'OK, fine,' I said, although my anxiety was so bad I could have happily thrown the number in the bin and moved to Australia.

I dialled the number slowly, stalling. The phone rang out for some time. Nobody answered, and no voicemail kicked in. Phew.

'No answer,' I shrugged at Swanson.

'Did it ring?' He crossed his arms and leant back in the chair. I nodded.

'Should I try?' he said, after a moment's silence.

'Feel free,' I passed him the piece of paper.

Swanson rang the number and stared at me for a moment with the phone to his ear. He shrugged.

'No answer. I'll call the low security unit tomorrow,' he said eventually, 'to see if he's been back.'

'Will you arrest him?'

'I'm not sure what he's done yet. We know he didn't shoot Harry, but Astrids accused him of bringing the gun into the house. We will need to at least question him.' He looked away to the kitchen door.

I nodded. There was nothing I could do if my brother had broken the law. Though how the hell he would know where to get a gun from or why he'd threatened Astrid with one was beyond me.

'Hart will probably wonder where I am. We're working late.' He glanced at the kitchen door again.

'OK. I need to go shopping, anyway.'

I led him to the front door, and he swept past me to get through, gently brushing against my shoulder. He mumbled a sorry and turned to look at me in the doorway. We stared at each other, just for a moment, and then he was gone.

I stared into the empty corridor, wishing I could call him back to stay with me. Usually, I welcomed being alone, but not tonight. Having Swanson around, even for a few minutes, had felt nice.

I shoved my feelings to one side and closed the door, and then went back to the kitchen to sit with my head in my hands. Tiredness stung my eyes but I knew I wouldn't be able to sleep anytime soon.

If my brother wasn't in the hospital, then where would he go?

Presumably, he had a plan before he went to Astrid's house. I just needed to figure out his next steps, which was nearly impossible without knowing why he went there in the first place.

Who else did Eddie know?

Panic flooded me as I realised where else he might go.

I jumped up and grabbed my bag and keys, and ran down the stairs to the car park. I tried to call Mum as I ran, but she didn't answer. There was barely any point in her having a mobile phone. I threw the phone on to the front seat and sped out of the car park.

Mum lived twenty minutes away in the old mining town of Ilkeston. I weaved in and out of traffic as much as I could, cursing the ridiculous fifty miles-per-hour speed limit and the roadworks on the A52. I called her again as I drove, yet still there was no answer. My legs felt like a dead weight as I maneuvered the pedals. *What would Eddie do to Mum?*

She still lived in the same house where he attacked her all those years ago. I'd begged her to move repeatedly — especially after last year. I tried calling Swanson instead, but he didn't answer. I left him a short voicemail asking him to call me ASAP.

I pushed on through Spondon, slowing for the speed cameras until I reached Dale Road and hit seventy miles-per-hour.

Despite the roadworks and cameras, I made it to Mum's house in less than fifteen minutes. I pulled up in front of her small driveway and slammed on the brakes. Mum's front door was half open.

I grabbed my phone and left the car door open for fear of making too much noise. Sneaking out onto the pavement, I crept up the drive to the front door.

My body froze a foot away from the door. I felt eleven years old again, hiding under the table and listening to my brother break down the front door.

I shook the feeling away. There were no excuses as an adult, and I had to make sure Mum was OK. I took another step towards the open front door, but stopped when I heard an animated voice coming from inside.

'That's all I came to say. I'm sorry. I spend my life making other people say sorry now too, Mum, and I'm going to make you proud of me. Maybe one day you will forgive me.'

Eddie. Hearing his voice threw me. He sounded calm. He wasn't about to hurt her. Maybe he really was better.

Guilt tugged at me. Here I was calling the police on him just like I did all those years ago, when Eddie was just trying to make up for what he had done.

He didn't even know about Marinda's lies yet.

I heard Mum respond, but her voice was too quiet for me to hear her words.

Eddie responded to whatever Mum had said to him. 'No. It was my fault. I'm going now. *Don't* look for me. You're better off without me. I could get sick again at any moment.'

Footsteps headed towards the front door, and a jolt of fear ran through me. I ran to the left of the front garden and knelt by the tall fence which led to the back garden path. I wasn't ready to face Eddie, so I watched instead as the brother I'd spent twenty years looking for walked away.

He was shorter than I remembered, with thinning light hair. I hadn't realised that Eddie would be forty-one years old now, not the strapping twenty-one-year-old I remembered.

He stopped at my car with its partially open door, and craned his neck to look left and right down the street. My heartbeat quickened, though he didn't look behind him. He walked down the street instead and took a left turn.

I slipped down to the bottom of the driveway to watch him go; he walked to the end of the street and took a right.

A sudden urge to hug my big brother overtook me, and my feet pounded the pavement as I raced to the bottom of the street.

I bent over and sucked in deep lungfuls of air. I looked left, and saw nothing. I ran to the end of that street too, but he'd disappeared. Shit. Why didn't I stop him when I had the chance?

I ran back to Mum's, sweating and red faced by the time I reached her. The front door was still ajar. Inside, I found her on the sofa, tears streaming down her face. I rushed over and threw my arms around her.

'Are you OK? Did he hurt you?' I asked.

She shook her head.

'I'll make you some tea and then you can tell me what happened, OK?' I didn't wait for a response. My hands shook as I poured water into the kettle.

'Do you take sugar, Mum?' I called, feeling guilty for not knowing how she took her tea. I couldn't remember ever making her one.

She sniffed and sat forward in her chair, attempting to pull herself together. 'Two please, love.'

A few moments later, we had both stopped shaking and Mum was sipping her tea. It's amazing what a cup of tea can do for people.

'How was he, Mum?'

'He was… calm,' she shrugged, 'he didn't make much sense. He said he's sorry for hurting me and he just wants to help people get better by taking responsibility for their actions. I'm not sure what he was talking about. I guess he feels guilty.'

'I saw him earlier. In the kitchen of a lady's house. Her name was Sophie. She changed it to Astrid. I'm still not sure what he was doing there.'

'How does he know her?' Mum asked.

'I hoped you could tell me. She went through something years ago. Her husband abused her. She snapped and stabbed him. She seems to have forgotten what happened. She tells everyone her ex was amazing, as if she's blocked out all the abuse.'

'Oh, well, lots of women lie to others about domestic abuse. It's rare they broadcast it.'

'No, she apparently believes it. But I don't know her, so…' I shrugged.

'Was Eddie trying to help her to remember?'

'I honestly don't know.' I hoped Eddie was trying to help Astrid, but how on earth did he know about her or her past? He'd been locked away. It made no sense.

We fell silent as Mum drank her tea. Her hands looked frail against the mug.

'Does he know about Marinda?' I asked.

'I don't know. I didn't want to upset him, love. I suggested it was Marinda at fault and he told me no, it was his.'

'He needs to be told when he's in a safe environment.' I agreed.

My mobile phone rang, its shrill noise making us both jump. I pulled it from my pocket. It was Swanson returning my call.

My finger hovered over the 'accept' button, yet I clicked 'ignore'. The only thing I knew for sure was that I had to find my brother, and I wanted to do it alone.

Swanson

Swanson raced back to the office as fast as the speed limits and road works allowed. Hart would probably accuse him of disappearing again. Sure enough, her name flashed up on his caller ID a few seconds after he pulled out of Summer's car park.

She didn't even bother saying hello. 'Where the hell are you now?'

'On my way. I got stuck behind a slow truck. You know, the ones that spray stuff off the back. I wasn't risking a chip in my bonnet.'

'Oh. Well, be quick. The most recent DNA results are back in for the sick bastard that's been attacking these girls. We got a hit.'

'Shit, really? Who is it?' he sat up straight in the driver's seat, ignoring the tug of the seat belt.

'If you were here, you'd know.' Hart hung up the phone.

Swanson cursed out loud and put his foot down. He overtook an old woman in a Micra and sped towards the office. He knew exactly where the speed cameras were and how to avoid them. The rain pelted down now and mammoth puddles engulfed parts of the road.

He flew into the office car park a few minutes later and

skidded to a halt in someone else's parking spot. *Fuck it.* He wouldn't be there long.

His phone rang again as he exited the car, and Summer's name flashed up. He silenced her call and sprinted into the office to find Hart. The Ops room was a whirlwind of activity and noise. Hart stared at him from her seat at his desk with a smug look on her face.

'Thought that would get you here,' she said, making no effort to move out of his seat.

'Yeah, yeah. You got me, Robin. Spill, then.' He took the chair next to his own and swivelled it to face her.

'Here you go.' She turned a computer screen towards him, and a profile of a man showed up.

Swanson stared at the picture with his mouth half open.

'You OK?'

Bile sat in the bottom of his stomach. He closed his mouth and swallowed hard to make sure it stayed down. He cleared his throat to sound normal. 'Yeah, fine. Where does he live then?'

'No idea. Last known address was 69 Mill Street, Ashfield. So what the hell is he doing around here?'

'Has anyone been to Ashfield to check on him yet?' Swanson asked.

'We're waiting to hear from the local guys. They're going to check it out. Murray's doing a brief in a minute.'

As if hearing her name, Detective Chief Inspector Murray walked into the office. DCI Murray was a secret crush for most people in the force, but not for Swanson. She was alright, but had the worst resting bitch face, and it suited her personality.

As soon as she noticed Swanson sitting in the middle of the room she strode straight up to him. He cursed himself for not being smaller. He could never bloody hide in a room.

'Where have you been?' She gave him a steely look with bright blue eyes.

Swanson felt his face redden.

Hart was going to take the piss for a long time.

'With Hart at the hospital, boss.' He looked at Hart, and she nodded once to confirm.

'Before that?' Murray raised an eyebrow.

'I got a call from someone who thought they had information on the shooting earlier today, boss.' He looked back at Murray, trying to meet her gaze. As if it couldn't cut through glass.

'And did they?'

'I think so, boss. Just checking it out. I'll update soon.'

'You can update me as soon as I finish this briefing and it will get passed on. I want to know what was worth disappearing from the worst serial rape case Derby has ever seen.' Her heels thudded against the grey carpet as she walked to the front of the briefing room. Hart stared after her, clearly looking at her arse.

'You fancy her,' Swanson said.

'I do not. You do! Oohh yes boss, let me in your pants please boss,' she whispered in a stupid voice.

'Fuck off. She's not my type. I prefer them *less* bitchy. Like you.' he stifled a laugh.

Hart slapped his arm.

Swanson didn't laugh for long. Over Hart's shoulder, the face stared back out at him from the computer screen. The sick feeling returned. 'I actually think... I'm gonna throw up.'

'You look white.' Hart gave him a strange look, 'Go to the toilet. Don't throw up here.'

Swanson snuck out of the room whilst DCI Murray had her

back turned. He ran down the corridor to the men's toilets, and once he'd made sure no one was inside, he whipped out his phone and returned Summer's call. No answer. He sent her a quick text, and rang Sophie instead. His heart was hammering. She didn't answer either. Christ, how was he supposed to make sure they were OK if neither of them answered? He rubbed his face with his hands. He needed to get out and check on Sophie, first.

Because the face staring out from the computer was Benjamin Bates.

Astrid

Over the years, I'd imagined this very day in my head again and again. Ben and I reunited, at last. I would be safe again in his arms.

Yet instead of feeling safe, my fear towered over me, a vast shadow bigger than I'd ever seen it. I watched it grow over the ceiling, and down the rear wall. A cascade of memories flooded me as I looked at Ben, and terror hit me like a brick.

'Hi, babe.' Ben smiled at me. 'How have you been enjoying your life without me?'

Instead of running to him, as I had so many times in my dreams, I took a step back. My heart wanted to go to him. My body told me to run. I blinked hard, trying to stop the memories: fear, love, pain. Tears ran down my cheeks.

'Hey.' Ben stood and walked over to me. He was a whole foot taller than me. I tried to retreat further, but my back hit the side of the staircase. He reached me in seconds and towered above me. For the first time in so long, I could smell him again. My Ben. He reached out his thumb and wiped the tears from my cheeks. 'It's OK. I'm back now.'

I sank into his arms and let the tears flow. Too many feelings fought inside me, and I couldn't tell which ones to listen to. The shadow grew in each corner of the room and blocked out any light. Darkness surrounded me.

I needed to get out. 'This is too much,' I pulled away from his embrace and turned to walk away, with no clue of where to go. He grabbed my arm and pulled me back into his arms.

'Shh, it's OK. I've got you now.' His arms tightened further around me.

'Ben, you're hurting me.' I wriggled, trying to get out of his grip.

'It's OK,' he whispered, squeezing tighter, 'I just missed you. Didn't you miss me?'

I nodded my head, unable to speak. I struggled to draw a breath.

'You don't look like you missed me.' He released his grip a little and stuck out his bottom lip.

I said nothing, but took deep breaths. The shadow covered the entire living room. 'Do you see the darkness?' I asked him.

He laughed. 'All I've seen is darkness after what you did to me.'

'What I did?' My voice trembled. A memory of being thrown on a bed flashed in my head.

'Did you really think I would never find you?' he asked.

'What? I hoped you would find me. We looked for you for a long time.'

'We?' His face changed instantly. 'You mean the son you stole from me?'

'Our son!' I couldn't help but raise my voice. 'Officer Swanson and the police. Me and Harry, too.'

'Officer Swanson? Officer Swanson made me disappear!' He raised his voice. 'After you stabbed me, you ungrateful fucking bitch.'

'What are you talking about? I'd never stab you!' The room

swayed. I leant back against the staircase and closed my eyes. 'Swanson looked for you for years.'

'Swanson found me after you stabbed me with those damn nail scissors. He drove me to the hospital and threatened to throw me in prison if I came back. Even though you were the one who attacked me! *I* was the victim and he treated me like shit.'

I shook my head. 'That's not true.'

'Are you calling me a liar?' His face darkened.

'No! How did you find me now? Has Kai seen you?' I asked.

'Easy. I found out where Swanson was based and followed him around for a bit. I was watching some old woman he knows, and you turned up at her house.'

'Old woman? Do you mean Barb?'

'Yep, think so. I followed you home weeks ago.' He grinned, 'Kai still lives where he used to, with that slut of a mother. I just left him a note. I thought he'd seen me when I was walking away but I'm not sure.'

'You left me that note?'

'I wrote the note and gave it to Eddie. He gave it to Harry. Harry didn't know what it said. But he knows the truth now thanks to Eddie!'

'Eddie? That's what that woman called Charles earlier.' Even in my panicked state, I knew I needed to keep him talking. Maybe the darkness would take him.

'Yep. My nuthouse friend. I met him doing a job at his place. He's not all there. Even so, he helped me. I told him you killed my friend and needed to pay. I've got friends everywhere, Sophie. Have you forgotten that?' He grinned, yet it was more menacing than a direct threat.

'He was with Harry earlier? You let someone who's mentally

206

ill take Harry?' Flashes of blood and scissors and screaming ran through my mind.

'I was watching the whole time! He wouldn't have hurt Harry. Had to have someone watching you who you wouldn't recognise. At least until it was time for you to pay for what you did.'

'Make me pay? For what?'

'Don't act so fucking coy with me.' His face twisted into ugly rage and that was it, that was the face.

The memory flooded back to me and I pushed him away. 'You fucking rapist,' I spat.

My face exploded with pain as his fist connected with my cheek. The hard floor smashed against my face. His foot connected with my stomach, the taste of blood metallic in my mouth.

'Harry is my son, bitch. And I'm taking him with me. He knows all about you now, doesn't he?' he growled.

The thought of him taking Harry made me retch. The full memory of stabbing Ben overwhelmed me. Blood dripping all over our home came flashing back, and the panic that I'd felt as I ran away.

I thought he was dead. Swanson told me he was gone. Swanson lied.

'Leave Harry alone!' I shouted.

His hands wrapped around my throat in an instant. 'Harry will be well looked after and you'll never get the chance to hurt me again, bitch.'

He flipped me over as if I weighed nothing and his hand reached up my dress to pull down my leggings. He forced my head down onto the hard floor and his knee pushed my leg to the side. Every memory of him hurting me came back to me, and I remembered what I'd done. But with my face in the ground, I couldn't see the Arracht. I couldn't hear its guttural noise.

I was alone again, and I was going to die.

Summer

There was only one other person I could think of who might know something about Eddie, and that was Sophie. He'd been in her house, though I had no idea why. She must know something about him. Sophie didn't live far from me: she was just on the other side of the city. It didn't take long to get to her.

I pulled up on her road and got out of the car, leaning against the bonnet for a moment. I didn't even know what to say to her. *Should I admit he is my brother?* It was unlikely she would want to help him — or me — if she knew. She was probably still at the hospital, anyway, asleep with her son.

Fuck it. I crossed the road and readied myself to talk to her in case she was inside. But as I reached the front gate, I noticed her front door stood wide open. *Shit.* I snatched my phone from my coat pocket and dialled Swanson. Thankfully, he finally picked up.

'Look, I'm at Astrid's — or Sophie's — house… whatever her name is.'

'Why? It's a crime scene, Summer. You need to leave.'

'Don't interrupt! Her front door is wide open. I don't know what to do.'

'Jesus fucking christ. Do nothing. I'll be there in five

209

minutes.'

I put the phone down and stared at the door. 'Astrid?' I called as loud as I could, hoping I would scare off any bad guys. *Like my brother?* I heard a shout and instinctively ran to the front door, but stopped in my tracks as I reached it. I turned to see if anyone else was around, and saw no one. So, instead, I peered through the front door. 'Hello?' I called.

'Summer!' a male voice called. A voice which made me want to run away from it and towards it simultaneously.

'Eddie?' I walked inside and immediately spotted Astrid sitting on the floor of the living room. Blood poured down her tear-streaked face. She turned her head towards me, but didn't appear to see me.

Eddie stood in the middle of the living room, and a man I didn't recognise lay on the floor. I looked up at Eddie. His face was a whirlwind of confusion.

'Jesus, Eddie. What did you do?' I stepped backwards.

'I...I... was trying to help,' he said. Tears streaked his cheeks.

'You saved me,' Astrid stood shakily, holding on to the wall for support. She looked at him, and then back at me. 'He saved me.'

'What happened?' I said to Astrid, but brought my gaze straight back to Eddie. This wasn't the reunion I had in mind.

'Ben came back. He came back,' Astrid muttered.

'He was hurting her,' Eddie pointed to the man on the floor.

'You stopped him?' I asked.

Eddie nodded. His hands were shaking. His eyes darted all over the room. He wanted to run.

'Hey, Eddie. It's OK. Look at me.' I smiled at him. 'Do you recognise me?'

He nodded. 'Summer.' It was barely more than a whisper.

'I'm sorry, Summer.'

'It's OK, Eddie. Do you know that man?' I asked.

'Yes. The electrician.' He pointed to Ben. 'He said she had his friend's son. He said she killed his friend and she was ill and Harry needed saving.'

'He's a liar,' Astrid said.

'The electrician?' I asked.

'Yes, he was doing a job at the…' He glanced at Astrid. 'At my house. He said he knew you, Summer.'

'He knew me?' I said. 'I've never seen him before, Eddie.'

Eddie smashed his fist into his own forehead over and over. I ran to him and gently took his hand, just as Swanson's large form appeared in the doorway. He surveyed the room and went to Astrid first.

'Are you OK?' he asked her.

She looked up and around the room. A smile spread across her face. 'The darkness.' She gave a short laugh.

Swanson glanced at me with worried eyes. 'The darkness?' He turned back to her.

'It's gone.' She laughed again.

'Good, I'm glad it's gone. Is your head OK?' Swanson asked her.

She nodded.

'OK, good. Help is coming.'

Swanson moved away from her and over to the man on the floor, he lifted his wrist to check his pulse. 'What happened to him?' he asked.

'He was hurting her.' Eddie had stopped punching himself and looked lost, like an overgrown child. 'I need to go now, Sir.'

Tears stung my eyes. My brother *wasn't* the bad guy. He was

OK. He just wanted to help. Eddie moved to leave, and I pulled him back gently. 'You can't go, Eddie. The police will need to talk to you.'

He shook his head vehemently. 'No. No police.'

I looked at Swanson, who glanced at Eddie before turning to me. He nodded his head slightly. I took the hint. I leaned up to whisper in Eddie's ear.

'Run home, Eddie. I'll come and see you tomorrow.'

Eddie braced himself, took a deep breath, and ran.

Swanson didn't move. 'Too dangerous to leave this suspect alone with you two. Priority is ensuring he's OK, and then arresting him.'

I nodded and allowed hope for Eddie to replace the fear in my heart. Maybe we really could be one big happy family again.

The man stirred and groaned from the floor. 'Take Astrid away, Summer,' Swanson called to me.

I held a hand out to Astrid. Fresh blood still trickled down her pale cheek. 'Come on, we need to go,' I told her.

She didn't move. She stared at the man, and didn't seem to hear me at all.

'Easy, now,' Swanson said to the man as he tried to sit up.

I had to get her out before he saw her. What was her boy's name? I tried to rack my brain.

'Astrid? We need to check on Harry.'

Her head snapped around at the mention of Harry, and she grabbed my hand. She leant her shaking body against mine as we walked outside. A car pulled up once we reached the bottom of the drive, and DI Hart jumped out. A marked police car pulled up behind her. Thank God Swanson had let Eddie leave. Now, I just needed to hope he'd gone home.

Astrid

The next morning I was sitting in the hospital waiting room. Harry was being checked over before they released him. It wouldn't be long before I got to take him home, wherever home would be.

Ben was alive. The police had arrested him, but he was alive.

And I felt more scared than ever. Repressed memories had hit me like a truck. Except this time, I was a different person. As a mother for over a decade now, I knew I had to fight back for Harry's sake. I was more prepared after being a lone parent for eleven years. I was stronger; I had money, and I had a career that I could do from anywhere in the world. And Harry. What else could I ever need?

I had to hurry. The police would arrive to question me again as soon as they knew Harry was well enough to talk to them. God knows what they'd charge me with. I knew even Alex couldn't get me out of this mess. Blaming Eddie was wrong, especially after he saved me from Ben. Yet I would do anything to be with Harry, and if an innocent man had to go to prison then so be it. My ringing phone broke my trail of thought. It surprised me to see Alex's name pop up.

'Hi, So... Astrid,' he said.

'Hi, Alex.'

'Ben's still here. I'll let you know if he gets released,' he said matter-of-factly, as though I were a normal witness. My stomach flipped at the mention of Ben's name.

'OK. What has he said?' I wasn't sure if I wanted to know what lies he was spewing, but I needed to protect myself from whatever he said about me.

'Everything. Ben's singing like a canary, trying to get less time and blame everything on Eddie. He's accused Eddie of stalking Summer,' He let out a low, short laugh.

Good. If he was blaming Eddie, too, I might get away with it.

'Was he stalking her? She knows him, right?'

'Stalking Summer? Maybe a little. I haven't spoken to him yet. He's her brother.'

'Oh, I see. How did Ben know Eddie was her brother?' I grabbed a pencil from my drawing table and jotted down what Alex said.

'He doesn't. He saw photos of Summer on Eddie's desk when Ben was doing a job there. Ben had seen Summer and I together in a cafe so he knew Eddie and I were connected.'

'Oh. Are you two seeing each other?'

I heard a strange noise from his throat. 'Er, no. No, we're not. We're little more than professional acquaintances, really.'

He was lying. 'I think you'd make a nice couple. Do you think Ben will get away with it?'

'No. He... we got a DNA match for another crime. He will go away for a long time.'

'Another crime? What?' I noticed he ignored my comment about them making a nice couple.

'I can't say at the minute, but trust me, they will lock him up for years.'

'You lied to me. You said he was dead.' A memory played in my mind of Alex returning from the house all those years ago. He'd been gone for ages, and he had blood on his shirt.

'No, I said he was gone. I didn't say he was dead.'

We fell into silence. I heard his breathing down the end of the phone, then he let out a loud sigh. 'Do you know a Peter Johnson, by the way?' Swanson asked.

'Yes. Ben's Dad. They don't really talk. He came out as gay years ago and it embarrassed Ben,' I said, realising Ben was never the person I thought he was.

'Does Peter work as an electrician as well?' Swanson asked.

'No, just Ben, but he sometimes used Peter's name for cash-in-hand jobs. He was paranoid about being found out for his taxes or something,'

'I see. Look, I can't call you anymore,' Swanson said, 'the investigation… it all needs to be legitimate. No one can find out what happened before. I'd lose my job for not reporting it. Do you understand?'

'I understand. You've done enough for me. I won't land you in it, and I won't call you again, I promise.'

'If you need anything, call Barb. She will help you.'

'OK. I will.'

I put the phone down and immediately went back to Google. Harry and I were finally going to move away and forget this whole nightmare. Maybe a caravan, or our own motorhome. Then we could go where we wanted, and we'd always be able to get away.

Just Harry and I together, our little family would be safe at last.

Summer

Eddie had gone missing again. He didn't return to the hospital. Probably because he was too scared of being sent back to high security Adrenna after what he'd done. I didn't blame him, that place gave me the creeps and I was just visiting. He was trying to help, but being violent meant he would get sent back regardless, and with Astrid saying the gun was his, poor Eddie stood no chance. I could only imagine he was walking around lost somewhere. Swanson said the police would check with the homeless community, as they at least needed him for questioning.

Worry gnawed at me as Joshua and I ate jam sandwiches and played a game on his Xbox. It wasn't a good combination, and my fingers were sticky from the spilt jam on the controller.

'What do I do now?' I asked him.

'I told you, Mummy! Now you come out of creative mode and go to the nether and attack,' he threw his hands around, exasperated I couldn't get the hang of his game.

'Oh, I think you'll be better than me at that bit.' I played on his ego and passed him the control.

'Yes, I will be.' He nodded without a hint of modesty.

I laughed and walked over to the dining table in the corner of the living room to check my phone, which was sitting on charge. There was a message from Swanson waiting for me:

'We haven't found Eddie. Will let you know when I have more info.'

I sat at the table and considered my options again. I'd spoken to Mum a few times since yesterday to make sure she was OK and to see if Eddie had turned up. She hadn't seen him.

Neither of us had spoken to Dylan yet. You'd think we'd be closer than we were, growing up just the two of us with Mum, and the shared tragedy of losing our father and brother in different ways. Yet I saw Dylan only two or three times a year. Every Christmas, and some birthdays. We tagged each other in the odd social media meme, but that was it. He lived forty minutes away in Mansfield. It may as well have been the other side of the country.

I scrolled to his number and let my finger rest there for a moment, not knowing what to say. I loved seeing him at Christmas, but it was so unusual for me to call out of the blue.

What would he think? He'd assume the worst. I pressed call before I thought about it too much and put the phone down altogether.

He answered on the second ring. 'Hello? Summer?'

'Hey, Dylan.' My anxiety eased now I could hear his voice.

'Are you OK? Is Mum OK?' he asked in a high-pitched voice.

'Yes, yes, we're fine!' I cut him off before his panic increased.

'Oh, good. Is it someone's birthday?' he asked.

'No. Dylan! Listen, I have something to tell you. It's about Eddie.'

'Eddie?'

I could almost see him scratching his brain. We never mentioned Eddie. It was an unwritten rule.

'Yeah. You know, our big brother,' I said.

217

'Yes, I know who Eddie is, Summer! I'm just surprised to hear you mention his name.'

'Yeah, well. He's sort of… back.' I put my head in my hands. This isn't how I should tell him.

'Back?'

'Yes. It's a long story, to be honest.' My fingers played with an elastic band that had been abandoned on the table at some point. How was I going to explain all of this?

'Is he there with you?'

'No, not yet. He's been following me, I think. I don't think he's dangerous now. Did Mum tell you about Marinda?'

'No. What do you mean he's been following you?'

'Oh, well, we have more to talk about than I thought,' I sighed.

'Right, I'm coming over. Text me your address.'

And with that, he hung up on me. I don't know what I had expected Dylan to say, but *not* that. I texted him my address and put the phone back on charge. A notification flashed up from Facebook as I was about to walk back to Joshua.

Charles Thomas wants to send you a message.

I gasped. Dad's name popping up on Facebook was not something I ever expected to see. I clicked 'view' and a message from Charles Thomas, a profile with no picture, popped up on the screen.

'I'm going to stay away. Nice to see you happy. Don't look for me.'

Eddie. I stared at the message as if looking at it would tell me what to do next. I needed to reply.

'Hi, Charles. It's OK, you don't have to run away. The police know it was all a big misunderstanding.'

But as I clicked send, the profile changed to 'Facebook user' and the message failed. He'd deleted the profile. I threw the

218

phone down on the table and put my head in my hands.

'You OK, Mummy?' Joshua shouted from the sofa without taking his eyes off his computer.

'Yes, honey. Just dropped my phone,' I sat up to look at him, engrossed in his building game. A part of me still wanted to stay away from Eddie. That part grew when I looked at Joshua. I knew deep down that wouldn't happen. I couldn't abandon my brother.

Now I had seen Eddie, and knew how lost he was, I was no longer scared of him. But he could hurt someone else if a person like Ben Bates took advantage of him again. I needed to know where he was, and how his mind was. He needed someone to look out for him.

Once Dylan was here, we could make a plan together. He could help me. We'd help Eddie together. One big happy family for the first time in twenty years. We would keep Eddie safe together, as a family should do.

Also by Ashley Beegan

Pre-order book three in the series now!

'The dogs always bark,
  And the violets die a death,
  When the devil brings the dark,
  And when he gets inside my head.'

Summer Thomas is fighting for her life after coming face to face with the devil of Adrenna Psychiatric Hospital.

It's up to DI Alex Swanson to find out the truth behind what happened to her, and he needs to be quick if he wants to save others from meeting the same fate.

But with his health deteriorating, past demons haunting him, and the devil himself close by, he might not survive long enough to save anyone.

He might end up meeting the devil himself.

Made in United States
North Haven, CT
15 August 2022

22771946R00136